ONLY YOU

ONLY YOU

•

Joye Ames

AVALON BOOKS
NEW YORK

PRINTED IN THE UNITED STATES OF AMERICA
ON ACID-FREE PAPER
BY HADDON CRAFTSMEN, BLOOMSBURG, PENNSYLVANIA

For our editor, Veronica Mixon,
Philip, and the Avalon staff.
Thanks, guys.

Chapter One

Ashley Bannister searched the restaurant with anxious eyes. The lopsided wooden door banged shut against her hip, making her take a short step forward. It was early for lunch but already a crowd of loud construction workers had gathered in the tiny diner.

The music from the jukebox blared out a rowdy country song punctuated by short bursts of laughter. The machine was placed conspicuously in the middle of the green tile floor. The lunch tables were covered by green-and-white-checkered cloths with wooden ladder-back chairs pulled out around them.

It wasn't hard to find him. He was sitting at the bar that wrapped around one side of the diner. His dark hair was tied back at the nape of his neck in a ponytail. Broad shoulders led down to a well-muscled back. Long legs were encased in sturdy jeans. He wasn't as

1

dusty as the two men seated on either side of him. No dirty sand spattered his boots. He turned to the man on his right and laughed at some joke the three men had shared.

Ashley remembered him as an attractive man. The years since she had seen him hadn't lessened that impact. She hadn't remembered him being quite so large. It made her task seem even more daunting.

Not that it mattered, she considered, straightening her shoulders under her pale yellow suit. She was there to see Trey Harris on business.

She'd only taken one step forward when the construction worker at Trey's side nudged him and nodded in her direction.

Trey picked up his glass, turned his head, and glanced at her. Surprise was quickly replaced by a cold, blank mask on his cleanly drawn face. But he didn't look away.

Ashley forced herself to continue toward him across the dining area, between the tables and the jukebox. She clenched her teeth when his own perusal included everything about her from head to toe.

She hadn't felt so self-conscious since she was twelve years old and her mother had made her enter a Junior Miss pageant! Her stomach tightened but pride kept her eyes locked with his.

"Trey Harris," she addressed him confidently. "I'm Ashley Bannister. I'd like to speak with you."

His gaze was malevolent. "I know who you are, Ashley. What do you want?"

Conscious of the audience around them as all ears perked up to hear their conversation, she smiled easily. It was a winning smile that had won her several beauty pageants. She practiced it again for his benefit that day.

''It won't take long,'' she answered readily, not losing her poise.

She had planned for days for that moment. She wanted to look her very best. If she could disarm him for a moment, she might get his attention.

His eyes flickered over her. Long, shapely legs. Dressed to be noticed. What was she after?

''All right.'' He gestured toward a table in the corner near the window. ''Come into my office.''

''Coffee, honey?'' the waitress behind the counter called out as they walked toward the table.

''No, thanks,'' she replied with a tight smile. She could feel curious gazes boring holes into her straight back as she followed him across the room.

Trey took a seat opposite her. His hands were wrapped around the glass he set before him on the table. His gray eyes were laden with storm clouds, and an angry mouth only hinted at his thoughts.

''You're looking well,'' she observed, fighting both herself and his frigid expression. She had thought that she was ready, but sitting across the table from him she wasn't so sure.

''Let's cut to the chase, Ashley. You haven't spoken to me for ten years. I've liked it that way. What do you want?''

"I want to hire you, Trey." Ashley wasted her carefully chosen speech and blurted out everything in the rush of a single sentence. "As a consultant."

Trey sat back from the table, a smile forming on his expressive face, his eyes half closing as though he'd swallowed a really good piece of pecan pie. Revenge was sweeter than anything he'd ever tasted.

He focused back on her, taking in all the ploys. Her pale blond hair curled at her shoulders, emphasizing her big blue eyes. He wasn't impressed.

He shook his head and smiled a breathtaking smile of his own. "So. You want to offer me a job?"

"Yes. Well, in a manner of speaking."

"Don't waver on me now, Ashley." His eyes quirked up at the corners. "You came on with all your guns primed. I think I know what a duck must feel like on the first day of hunting season."

Ashley swallowed on a suddenly dry throat and ached to smooth her skirt or pat her hair. Only resolve to gain his respect kept her still in her chair.

The sudden teasing light in his stormy eyes was unexpected. Trey Harris was turning out to be someone altogether different than she remembered. It had been a long time.

"All right," she began again with new confidence. "I am offering you a job. I know you aren't looking for one. I know you don't need one. But I need you."

"I'm flattered." He sat back in his chair again and studied her. "What is it you need me for?"

"You were the best at what you did for my father, Trey. I need the best."

He shook his head, wondering when he had ever had such a good time. "Ashley, I can't decide if you're trying to make me feel guilty or if you're stroking my ego."

She eyed his face steadily. "Bannister is in danger of losing its government contracts. With the competition from newer mills, the older firms don't look so attractive. We have a chance at a big contract with a Japanese company. We've been on the verge of turning this around. Then last week, Bill Raymond had a stroke."

Trey frowned. "Is he going to make it?"

Ashley shrugged and said sadly, "The doctors aren't sure yet. I know the two of you worked together for a while."

"He's a good man," Trey replied. *A much better man than your father,* he added silently.

"You know everything about the business, Trey. You and Bill and my father saved the plant ten years ago by making it profitable again. I know you could do it this time, too."

"It's been a long time, Ashley."

She took a deep breath. "If you could look over the situation. Tell me what I can do to make it work."

"I can save us both some trouble." He leveled her hopes with a quick glance. "Sell out. Make money before it's all gone."

"I don't want to make money," she replied earnestly.

"That's your loss." he pronounced. "Look, Ashley. I haven't done this kind of work in ten years. I don't know if I could help even if I had the time. I have commitments. Something like this can't be done in a day."

"All I'm asking is a few hours of your time," she argued. "I'd pay you well. If you couldn't help, you wouldn't have lost anything."

"You don't have enough money to make that offer attractive," he returned brutally, tiring of the game. "I have to go."

"Isn't there anything I can do that would change your mind?"

They stood up at the same time, almost the same height. That close, she could see the small lines in his face, fanning out from his eyes and around his mouth. He looked hard and cynical in a way that made her feel as though he were laughing at her. She wanted to reach out and take back those hastily spoken words as one mocking dark brow raised and his eyes appraised her lightly.

"What did you have in mind?"

"Give me an hour to explain my plan. I can change your mind."

He looked into her clear blue eyes so full of determination and Bannister pride. It was the moment he'd been anticipating for ten years.

"Dinner?" he proposed. He wasn't sure where that

came from. He hadn't planned it. Just the idea that she had asked for his help was supposed to be enough. He didn't plan on dragging out his game of cat and mouse for any longer than it took to tell her to get lost.

"Great!" She pounced without hesitation. "I could pick you up."

He shook his head. "I'll meet you at the plant at seven."

She nodded. "I'll be there."

"Good." He smiled at her. He couldn't wait. It was like Christmas in June. It was going to be even sweeter this way.

Ashley didn't respond, watching him walk away. He was possibly the only chance she had to save Bannister Manufacturing. She'd have to play the game his way.

She sank down slowly on the hard wooden chair, her knees feeling weak.

"Could I get something for you?" the waitress asked her.

"A big aspirin," she told her, not looking up.

The waitress, working her way through college, with a boyfriend her parents hated, understood the sentiment, if not the problem. She shrugged and left her there, going to check on her other tables.

It was too early to go home, even though Ashley wanted to hide her head under her pillows. She wasn't used to asking for help.

Instead, she took the long way back to the plant, phrasing and rephrasing what she would say to her assistant and the temporary plant manager. They were the only ones who knew she was going to talk to Trey Harris.

The idea to talk to the man had come from her assistant, Frances. The day after Bill's stroke, she had seen an article about Trey in the *Martinsville Gazette.*

"Isn't that the same Trey Harris who worked here a while back?"

"I think so." Ashley had barely paid attention, lost in her thoughts. "Why?"

Frances looked at her as though she were a slow child. "He was a good man, Ashley. He really knew what he was doing."

The plan was simple. It had been easy to find out where he was living. It had been a little harder to find a way to talk to him. It wasn't until Frances's cousin, whose uncle was the cook at Josie's Diner, had identified Trey Harris as the man who always ate lunch at the restaurant every Tuesday, that an encounter had seemed possible.

From there, Ashley had planned her assault.

Such as it was. She grimaced as she drove down the shaded streets. The tall oaks, easily a hundred and fifty years old, made a canopy against the bright, hot sun, protecting the old houses that lined the road.

That was one of the problems with Bannister Manufacturing, she decided, as well as Martinsville itself. Protected, sheltered against the sun, against time, against the outside world.

Or at least that was what everyone had thought.

When her great-grandfather had been the first man to pilot a hot air balloon to the coast and back, the Bannister family had become famous and made their fortune.

As time passed, they had prospered and her grandfather had built Bannister Manufacturing. It had been started to make the balloons that gracefully soared through the blue South Carolina skies. Later, they had begun making parachutes as well, the company staying fat and healthy on hefty government contracts, even in hard times.

She could remember her father shaking his head as he read the morning paper and her mother bustling around the kitchen. Martinsville was never touched by outside turbulence, and Bannister grew and retained its innocence of the world.

Ashley was an only child. A girl, at that. Her father had sighed over not having a son, then jumped in to bring the next Bannister into the business. For three generations, that was the way it had been done.

Parish Bannister had left his wife and daughter the year before with a beautiful old house that had been paid for a generation before Ashley's birth. Bannister Manufacturing had been flourishing, even though government contracts were a little smaller. The company was debt free; stockholders were happy. It seemed as though they would be cushioned through another generation.

Then, a month after Parish had died, leaving his only daughter at the helm of his grandfather's company, Bannister had lost several lucrative contracts. There was a little stockholder grumbling but Ashley had gone out in true Bannister fashion and secured a few new clients.

Then there were the ones she had lost. A few more, including a large government contract, were being held up in the decision-making process.

Ashley didn't realize that something was wrong until a few close friends of the family called to tell her that they had been approached to sell their stocks in Bannister. From that moment, it had been a nightmare.

A company less than a hundred miles away from Martinsville was competing with them, using newer equipment and methods. Some stockholders, disgruntled by the possibility of losses and lured by the chance to make money, sold out readily.

Ashley didn't panic at first. Things had slipped before but it had always worked out. She had gone about her job of running the company and tucked away her worries.

But many prospective clients saw the struggle as a sign that the company couldn't hold its own and wouldn't do business with them. A few others dropped their contracts. Bannister was struggling for the first time in its existence.

Ashley wasn't proud. She wished her grandfather was there to handle the crisis or that her parents had also had a son who was faced with the dissolution of the hundred-year-old company.

She could sell contracts and handle differences between employees, but she had relied heavily on Bill Raymond for the day-to-day running of the plant. He had been with her father for thirty years. She had never dreamed that he wouldn't be there for her.

Three hundred jobs. People with families, who had lived in Martinsville all of their lives, were depending on what she did to repair the damage done to the company. The mayor had told her over lunch that the consequences to the community would be disastrous.

Ashley realized that she had reached the plant when she looked up at the long, red brick building in the parking lot. In the sun, it looked every one of its years. The roof needed tarring and the windows needed cleaning.

Some of her workers were sitting outside at the picnic tables eating lunch. *So many people,* she thought unhappily. She felt as though she had let them all down.

Trey Harris was a long shot, but she was backed into a corner. There was nowhere else for her to turn. When she'd first thought about contacting him, every muscle in her body had turned to marshmallow. It had been such a long time and certainly he had no reason to do her any favors.

Ten years before, Trey Harris had been fresh out of college, full of promise and new ideas. Her father had hired him to learn the ropes at Bannister and eventually to take over for Bill Raymond.

He had learned quickly. In less than a year, he had Bannister running at peak operation. He was getting materials at lower prices and he had found new markets. The company had been ready to expand and hire new people when Ashley had come home with her new fiancé.

Parish Bannister saw the advantage of keeping the company in the family. For all that he had taught Ashley, there had always been something lacking that he held back from her. Ashley's future husband became the son life had never given him.

It wasn't long before Trey found more and more of his decisions challenged by Ashley's fiancé. More of his responsibilities were designated to the other man and finally he was formally demoted.

Infuriated by the callous treatment he had received at the hands of Parish Bannister, Trey had quit and taken several customers with him. He started his own company a few blocks away and he worked feverishly to compete with his previous employer.

Ashley gripped the steering wheel tightly as she recalled those terrible times. She had never known exactly what had happened. One day, Harris Manufacturing was thriving. The next, it had shut down. Trey disappeared for a few years. The customers he had taken had come back to Bannister.

To make matters worse, a month after Trey Harris had left town, Ashley's fiancé had decided that the business was not for him. Neither was she. She found him gone one morning. He had left her a note on their front door.

So, ten years later, she had gone to Trey for help.

He knew the business inside-out. She couldn't think of any reason that he would help her, except that Frances had remembered that he had been close to Bill Raymond.

He had appeared to be genuinely upset at the news when she had told him about Bill's stroke. She hoped the old friendship would bring him back. If not, maybe having a Bannister come to him for help would be gratifying.

Would it be enough? It had been a long time ago and she knew Trey had moved on with his life. Surely he couldn't hold more than a small grudge for that long. And she was only asking for a few hours. Just enough time to give her some ideas as to how she could salvage what was left of her company.

Ashley knew her options were limited if she couldn't win him over. She looked down at her short skirt and high heels and she knew it was probably hopeless if she'd thought that mere appearances would change Trey's mind.

What would her grandfather had done? She had no way of knowing. She guessed he would have done whatever it took to get what was needed to keep his people working. That was what she had done.

Ashley opened her car door and squinted into the sun. Whatever happened, she had done her best.

''Well?'' Frances barely waited until Ashley reached the office, holding the door open for her.

David Baxter, the warehouse manager whom she'd

made temporary plant manager, was waiting hopefully at the door as well.

"I talked to him," she told them. "He wasn't interested."

"That was it?" Frances demanded to know. She had been so sure he would be their hero.

"Not entirely," Ashley hedged, getting herself a glass of water from the cooler.

David set his purple-and-yellow Bannister cap back on his head. "I was afraid it wouldn't work."

"What did he say, Ashley?" Frances wanted to hear it all.

"He said we didn't have enough money to make it interesting for him and that we should sell the plant." Ashley walked to her father's old desk, now crammed with her belongings. She picked up her stack of mail and glanced through it. "Then he asked me to talk to him at dinner tonight."

"What?" Frances and David echoed together.

"It's just a meeting," she admitted. "It may not amount to anything."

Frances and David exchanged quick glances as Ashley looked down at the mail.

"That's wonderful!" Frances cleared her throat and adjusted her glasses.

"I hope so." Ashley looked up at them. "I'm just not sure."

"I gotta get back out there," David told her, looking at his watch. He'd only been warehouse manager there for about a year. He was still nervous about handling everything Ashley had asked of him.

"Did you see Bill today?" Ashley asked Frances, knowing they were all thinking of their stricken co-worker. He was only allowed two visitors a day, outside of his immediate family. So they took turns going to the hospital.

"Oh, Ashley." Frances sighed. "He doesn't recognize anyone. His wife told me this morning that they don't know if he'll ever walk again."

It was hard to imagine Bill, with his buoyant step and cheery smile, as the invalid they'd seen in the hospital.

David cleared his throat and gruffly told them that he had to go oversee the shift change. Frances blinked back tears from her faded blue eyes and answered her phone

Frances Anderson, who'd been Parish Bannister's assistant before he'd died, had seen his daughter grow up in the plant. She was sixty years old. Not quite ready or able to retire. Not able to easily go out and find another job. She needed the youngest Bannister to succeed. All they need was a miracle. She hoped Ashley could find one before it was too late.

Ashley had spent the day looking for one. She was the last person to leave the plant that night. She had a meeting with representatives from a Japanese group the following day and wanted everything to be perfect. She couldn't afford to lose the contract for making air bags for Tagami Corporation. It would either be another nail in her coffin, or a chance to hold on a little longer.

Trey found her there, hunched over her computer and a mountain of lists and files. He stood in the doorway, watching her run her fingers through her silky hair, not able to look away as she made a face at the computer, then smudged her lipstick with a careless hand.

She was a beautiful woman. A princess in this little town. He had to remind himself that he didn't like her any better than he liked her father. She was just as heartless. Just as certain that she would get her own way. He was just as determined that she wouldn't.

"Ashley?"

She turned from her computer screen and blinked to clear her blurred vision when she saw Trey's face. "Is it that late already?"

He smiled. There was a long black pen mark on her cheek. "It's seven-fifteen. I was in the parking lot waiting for you."

Her eyes flew open wide. "I'm sorry." Her hand went to her face. "Give me a few minutes to freshen up and we'll go."

But Trey had already been having second thoughts. He didn't need to have dinner with Ashley for him to tell her that he wouldn't help her. He could end it right there. "Let's just forget it, Ashley."

Her smile died. "You promised me a chance."

He glanced at her, then turned away. "I don't know what I was thinking."

Ashley put a hand on his arm. "Please, Trey."

He looked back at her, swearing that he saw tears standing on the full sweep of her pale lashes. He didn't want to be moved by her appeal. It was probably fake, anyway.

"You promised me dinner," she continued, not giving up.

"Ashley," he began, knowing that this was what he had wanted even though the aftertaste was bitter in his mouth when he looked at her. "I can't help you."

"Why?"

Why? With her standing that close to him, he wasn't really sure why. She'd had the same effect on him at the dinner that day. He shouldn't have given in then. He looked down at the dainty hand she had laid on his arm. Her fingernails were perfect ovals but there were smudges of ink on them.

Ashley looked at her hand, then quickly withdrew it. "Well," she said finally, her voice wavering only slightly. "We might as well have dinner. I made reservations."

He stared at her. "You're not making this any easier."

She held her head high. "That wasn't my intention."

Trey took out a clean white handkerchief and offered it to her, indicating that she had a lipstick smudge at the side of her mouth. "Fair means or foul, you'll get what you want?"

Ashley faltered, a fluttering in her chest making a

deep breath impossible as he continued to look at her. ''I always play fair.''

His eyes held hers as he made his decision. ''That must be why you need me.''

''I do . . . need you,'' she repeated breathlessly, feeling mesmerized by him. ''To—to save the plant.''

He felt her words down to his toes. Everything heated up at once. Even her mild qualification couldn't change that feeling. ''Dinner?''

She nodded, not trusting herself to speak.

''I'll wait for you in the car.

Chapter Two

Ashley hugged her side of the car and stared out into the darkening summer streets. Fair means or foul, he'd said. She stole a look at his handsome profile. He drove as intensely as he looked at her. She sensed that he would do whatever was necessary to get what he wanted. She didn't recall him being that way ten years before. He'd been brilliant when her father had hired him. He'd become ruthless since her father had driven him away.

Trey wasn't sure if he'd lost his mind or if he'd become so obsessed with Bannister, any Bannister, begging him for help that he was willing to go to extreme lengths to hear it. Either way, it wasn't something he needed in his life. Everything else was good. Everything was working. Until he let a Bannister into his life again. Suddenly, he felt like a man careening off the edge of a cliff, out of control.

They'd taken his car. He'd insisted. It was a way, however slight, to keep what control he could of a dangerous situation. The drive to the restaurant was too short for him. Once they were inside, he would have to look at her again and whatever insanity was possessing him would take over. He glanced furtively at her in the dark car interior. She was very still, very quiet. Like a china doll, he considered, wondering if it would be rude to let her off at the restaurant then back out on dinner.

"We're here," they both said when they had pulled into the parking lot. They looked at each other in the dim aura from the overhead lights, then looked away quickly.

Trey turned off the car's engine.

"Maybe this wasn't such a good idea," Ashley said quietly.

"Maybe not," he growled, opening the car door. "But we're here now and I'm hungry. Let's eat."

The restaurant was situated on the county line between a county that allowed wine sales and a county that didn't. In that way, the elegant little Italian eatery got the best of both worlds—the heavy traffic from Martinsville and the wine license from its neighbor.

The interior was dark and a little smoky from the candles that were on each table. The waiter found them a quiet, cozy booth and left them alone with the menu, convinced that they were a romantic couple. It was a small booth so that they were forced to sit closer together than either of them would have liked, yet neither of them asked for another table.

''What's good?'' Trey asked her, wondering if he had ever been as aware of a woman. Or as annoyed about it. Her perfume filled his senses. Her voice seemed to strike a chord of music in his ears. If he moved an inch to the right, he would be touching her.

''It's hot in here,'' she said, unbuttoning her yellow suit jacket, trying to maneuver away from him without being conspicuous. He was too close. She could barely breathe.

He watched in fascination as she removed the jacket and laid it carefully across the seat behind her. He realized that he'd thought all day about that neckline, wondering how such a prim little jacket could make a woman look so alluring. The white, sleeveless blouse she wore only added to the effect. It was demure, yet revealing, setting off Ashley's tanned arms and bright eyes.

Ashley felt his eyes on her and slowly folded her arms across her chest. Not that she had done anything to be ashamed of, she reminded herself. All she'd done was take off her jacket, but she felt exposed in front of him. His eyes seemed to see everything, to read her thoughts.

''The ravioli is good,'' she told him briefly, her eyes glued to the menu as though her life depended on it.

''I hate ravioli,'' he replied.

She glanced up at him but his face was hidden behind the menu. She looked at his hands on the menu. He had big hands, with long, tapered fingers. They reminded her that he was an artist, a sculptor, now. His life had changed since he'd worked for her father.

She remembered him being tall and very thin ten years before, she thought, glancing at the depth of his chest and the breadth of his shoulders. That had changed as well.

Ashley pushed her gaze back to the menu. What in the world was wrong with her anyway?

"The, uh, fettuccine is good," she said calmly.

"I hate fettuccine," he answered, without looking up at her.

They both sat silent after that. The music from the small trio near the center of the restaurant had drawn a few couples out to the dance floor. They were teen-agers, draped over each other, pressed as intimately as possible.

Ashley looked at them moving across the floor and cleared her throat uneasily. This was bad. This was *really* bad.

She looked up to tell him so and found him staring at her. Caught by the light in his gray eyes, she couldn't look away. They were alone, and she was falling toward him. . . .

"Wine?" the waiter asked, breaking the spell between them.

"No thank you!" they both answered at once.

They each drank from their water glasses and sat back in their places.

Ashley pulled up her courage and faced him. "Why were you staring at me?"

Trey looked away. "I was trying to see your father in you."

She shook her head. "We didn't look alike."

"I remember your mother," he said, thinking about the woman who had invited him to dinner at their house several times. "She was a gracious lady."

Her head went up. "Implying that I'm not?" she demanded.

"Implying that I don't recall you looking like her either."

"Oh."

"But you aren't," he added.

"A gracious lady?" she wondered, her grip tightening on the water glass.

"No," he replied. "You're a fighter. You don't mind getting down and dirty with the work. You screwed up your courage when you knew I had every reason to wipe the floor with you and you came after me anyway."

She sipped some water to ease her terribly tight throat. "Does that mean you'll help me?"

"No," he answered briefly. "It means I admire you. And under different circumstances—"

"Different?" she demanded, sitting forward. "You mean if you still didn't hate my father?"

His eyes danced lightly over her face. "Pretty much."

"You aren't hurting him by not helping," she reminded him. "He's dead. If it makes you feel any better, he was always sorry that you were gone. You were the son I could never be to him. He was miserable without you."

He looked at her, his eyes like polished steel. "Good."

Ashley put down her glass and stood up, taking her jacket with her. "I'm not hungry anymore. And I wouldn't want to pay the price you're asking for your help. Thanks anyway."

Trey watched her storm out of the restaurant. There *was* some Bannister temper in her after all, he decided. They had never had a chance to order dinner, but he left a big tip anyway and shrugged at the waiter, who commiserated with him over the loss of his lady.

She was white fire, shimmering with anger and righteous indignation. Her eyes had been like blue diamonds, as penetrating as lasers. And she was gone.

He looked around the empty parking lot, then checked the car, but she wasn't there either. Muttering about women and streaks of stubborn independence, he started the car and pulled out to the highway.

Ashley had already broken one of the fragile heels on her yellow shoes by the time he pulled up beside her. She didn't care. She would have broken her leg before she would get back in that car with him. She wasn't sure how far back it was to her home but she would get there without that evil, despicable man.

"Ashley," he said, the window zipping down on the passenger side as he pulled up beside her.

"Go away," she retorted, speeding up her pace despite her uneven gait.

"Ashley, we're two adults. We can disagree without you walking home."

"*I'm* an adult," she fumed. "You are a stupid, vengeful idiot!"

Trey pulled the car off the road about a hundred feet in front of her. He got out and slammed the car door, walking back to where she was limping along.

"Look, your father treated me like I was less than a man. He seemed to think I was his own private slave that he could dispose of when he was ready."

"I'm not going to argue with you about my father," she yelled at him. "He's dead now. He can't make it right with you."

"But you think I should help you save his company?" he demanded angrily.

"I think you should go away and leave me alone," she told him flatly. "I don't want your help. We'll get by without it."

"Sure you will," he taunted.

"I'd rather lose everything, *everything,* than have you help me!"

Trey took a deep breath. This was totally out of control. And it was starting to rain. "Ashley, we aren't going to work together, but that doesn't mean I can't drive you back to the plant. I'm sorry if your feelings are hurt. Let's just call it a night."

Ashley bent down, took off her shoes, then threw

them into the ditch that ran alongside the road. "Not if my life depended on it!"

Anger tore through Trey. The rain was coming down harder. He was already soaked. He wanted to pick her up and throw her into the car but reason and some vague sense of propriety that his mother had taught him made him turn around and get back in the car.

Ashley was glad to see the red taillights disappear over the next hill. It was raining more steadily. Fortunately it was a warm rain. The night was sultry with it. The grass was cool under her feet. But it was a long walk back. She took out her cell phone and dialed her mother's number.

It was busy. She tried a few friends who wouldn't demand an explanation about how she got out there that night. No answer. She tried calling Frances. Busy. Probably talking to her mother. She stuck the phone back in her purse.

She tried flagging down the next few cars that came up to her. They slowed but didn't stop. She wasn't surprised. Would she have stopped for some crazy woman walking alongside the road in the rain in the middle of the night?

Her anger had cooled considerably as she climbed to the top of the first hill. The wind had picked up and there was lightning in the distant darkness. What had she been thinking? She should have let Trey take her back to the plant. She wasn't really hot-tempered by nature. He had just pushed the right buttons.

She didn't blame him for not forgiving her father, she thought, beginning to walk a little slower. Parish had treated him like dirt. In his place, she was fairly sure that she would want to see his company collapse. She had hoped that he would be able to look past that to the people of Martinsville, but she should have known better.

Another car crested the hill and she tried to decide whether to flag it down and take her chances or walk for a few more hours. The car decided for her, though, slowing down and coming to a stop beside her. The door opened and she took a step back, sliding down on the wet grass.

A stifled screech came from her throat as she continued to slide down the muddy embankment. She finally came to rest at the bottom, half in a small runoff that had formed a creek in the rain. She couldn't catch her breath and her ankle hurt. Groaning, she started to get up.

''Ashley!'' a familiar voice called her name as two hands came out to help her.

''Trey?''

''Are you all right?'' he asked, finally managing to help her stand.

She yelped and leaned on one foot. ''I hate to say it,'' she told him, ''but I think I hurt my ankle.''

Rain burst furiously from the darkened sky. The thunder and lightning that had threatened now roared over the top of them like a freight train.

''We can't look at it here,'' he said. ''Hold on.''

Ashley yelped again as he lifted her in his arms and started back up the hill, but she held on to him. She didn't know how he could see where he was going between the bursts of lightning and the complete blackness of the night. She didn't care. He was warm and, while he wasn't dry, his arms were strong and sure around her. It was easy to forget that she had been angry at him.

He reached the top of the embankment. The car door was still open and he quickly put her inside.

"I'm ruining your car seat," she told him when he came around and got behind the wheel.

"Don't worry about it," he said breathlessly. He pushed his wet hair back from his face. "Are you in pain? Should I take you to the hospital?"

"No," she said calmly. "It's not that bad. If you could take me back to the plant—"

"I'll take you home," he told her firmly. "Do I need to lock the door?"

She looked at him in the close, dimly lit car. Water was still dripping from his face.

His cheekbones were prominent with his hair slicked back. He looked like he was frowning.

She shook her head. "I don't know what got into me. I'm usually more sensible."

He grimaced. "You don't look very sensible just now. Is that a cut?" He touched a dark streak down the right side of her face.

"I don't think so," she replied quietly, rubbing her hand against the place. "It's dirt. I'm covered in it."

"Me, too."

"I'll be fine," she continued as he didn't look away. His intent stare was unnerving her. "Really."

"I'm sorry, Ashley," he said. "I shouldn't have left you."

"What made you come back?" she wondered, even more curious about that question.

"I don't know," he admitted. "I should have just picked you up and put you in the car to begin with."

She smiled. "Then you would have had to lock the car door."

"And protect myself, huh?" He laughed shortly.

"And protect yourself," she agreed. "Is that a cut on your cheek?" She leaned forward slightly and touched the top of his cheek.

"It doesn't hurt," he repeated her words. Her hand resting against his face was doing crazy things to his pulse.

Ashley knew that she should move away. Her heart was pounding and she shivered. Not from the cold, because at the moment, she wasn't feeling cold at all. In fact, there was a decided warmth that had seeped along her spine and curled into her chest. Her hand moved across his cheek, caressing the warm, masculine skin beneath it.

Trey looked at her lips and couldn't look away. She was close to him, so close that he could see her pupils grow larger in her light eyes as he moved his head down to hers. It was ridiculous that he should want to kiss this stubborn, exasperating woman. He didn't like

her. He certainly didn't want to be emotionally involved with her. But he ached to feel her lips under
his, and, at that moment, it was all that mattered.

Ashley closed her eyes as he came closer. He was
going to kiss her. She didn't know why. She didn't
know why she wanted him to kiss her. But she did
want it.

She had expected . . . what? A short, quick kiss. A
moment of indulgence and then an hour of regret?

He didn't kiss her lips at first. He lowered his head
and his lips grazed her eyelids, tracing her feathered
brows, finding her temple and following the line of
her cheekbone. He whispered her name and touched
her hair. His mouth found the hollows in her face, the
curves in her smile, without fulfilling what she wanted.

He used his fingers as though he were a blind man,
memorizing the flawless skin and the subtle nuances.
He felt the pulse that beat in her throat and touched it
with his lips. He touched the worried frown that too
often graced her forehead, then smoothed a thumb
across the fullness of her mouth.

Ashley felt herself tremble. He gathered her closer.

"Cold?" he whispered.

"N-no," she managed. Words failed her. How
could she describe what she wanted? How she longed
to have him kiss her?

He kissed the side of her mouth. "You are so
beautiful."

"I, uh, I—"

"Shh." He helped her by touching his mouth to the other corner of her own. "You have wonderful lips."

Kiss me! she wanted to urge him. Instead she pushed her hands through his wet hair, bringing him closer.

He cradled her against him and finally, put his mouth on hers.

She was lost. It was as though each and every place his lips and fingers had touched pulsed with life and heat. Without conscious thought, she slanted her own mouth to meet his, tasting the rain on him.

She didn't know how long it lasted. She didn't think, didn't have time for regrets. When he finally lifted his head, she had entwined her hands around his neck. She was hanging on for everything she was worth. There was no tomorrow. No company to save. Only the two of them in a world that was so far removed from anything else she had ever encountered that she never wanted to go back again.

She opened her eyes slowly. He was looking at her as though he could tell everything about her from that kiss. She looked back at him, drowning in the deep seas of his eyes.

"I guess I should get you home," he said finally.

She nodded, not trusting herself to speak.

Ashley found that she didn't have to give him instructions to find her home. He remembered the way. It was just as well, because she wasn't sure if she could have given those directions. She was wet, muddy, and her brain had decided to go on vacation. All she could think about was his kiss.

The lights were blazing when he pulled his car around the circle drive, stopping in front of the house. The rain hadn't stopped and her mother was standing at the front door, urging her inside quickly.

"Thanks," Ashley said in a voice that sounded oddly strained even to herself. "For coming back for me."

"I'm sorry I left," he apologized again. "You got the better of me, Ashley. And you're right. I should have been over all of it a long time ago."

"Does that mean you'll help?" Her sluggish mind perked up at his words.

He smiled and shook his head. "Good night, Ashley. Do you need help getting inside?"

She shook her head as she got out and tested her weight on her foot. "It's okay. I'll be fine. Thanks." She felt like crying. Not because of her foot, or at least she didn't think so. Not because of her company or the rain or the mud. Or the passion she felt when he had kissed her.

Or maybe it was all of those things together.

"Who was that man?" her mother wanted to know as her daughter hobbled a little into the house and closed the door behind her.

"Trey Harris," Ashley told her blankly. "I fell down in the mud. Good night, Mother."

Her mother watched her daughter drift upstairs, wondering if it was too late to call Frances.

Ashley showered and fell asleep as soon as her head hit the pillow. She was awake early but drifted back to sleep again, thinking about her life and kissing Trey.

It certainly wasn't her first kiss but, as she dressed for work later, she considered that she led a sheltered life. She worked hard and didn't have time for much of a social life.

Maybe she should be thinking about other things, like being a mother and a wife. She was, after all, twenty-six years old. Not exactly a spring chicken, as her mother seemed to delight in telling her.

Her engagement to Johnny Thompson had been a very long time ago. She could remember that her heart was broken when he left her, but the pain hadn't been there for years.

She was mature, she told herself, looking at her reflection in the full-length mirror, adjusting the waist of her white skirt. She knew what she wanted from life. She touched up her discreet pink lip gloss, catching sight of her watch.

And she was late!

"Ashley!" her mother called out as her daughter ran down the stairs, picking up her briefcase as she headed for the door.

"I'm late, Mother. I'll see you later! I'm taking your car."

"Ashley, I need to talk to you!" her mother insisted.

"I'll call you from work!" Ashley promised, racing from the house.

It wasn't going to be her day.

The county had decided to work on the street outside her house. She waited patiently while the workers held out the stop sign. She followed the traffic slowly through the construction area, trying to avoid the debris.

Then she put her foot down hard on the gas pedal and flew down the quiet streets. No matter what she did, what shortcuts she took, Ashley was already ten minutes late by the time she reached the plant gates.

She pulled into her parking place, seeing Frances desperately trying to make conversation with the representatives from Tagami Corporation. Her car's brakes squealed as she stopped quickly, and all their heads turned.

"Good morning," she began, getting out of her car and running up the ramp to the front of the plant.

All three men's eyes glanced down at their watches, then back up at her face. No translation needed.

"Sorry I'm so late." She smiled and opted for getting it out in the open. "There was construction—"

The man in the middle, Mr. Matamori, translated her words for the other two, who nodded and smiled at her.

"Thank goodness you got here," Frances said with a grateful sigh.

"If you're ready then." Ashley nodded at her, then returned her gaze to the three visitors.

The tour of the plant went well. No machinery was broken down. Nothing was out of the ordinary. The three men were impressed by the productive workers and the cleanliness of the facility. They identified with David Baxter from the minute they met him.

The manager gave them each a Bannister cap and took them through the active hot air balloon section. One balloon, just being finished, was hanging from the high ceiling. The colors were breathtaking—bright blue overall, with an orange sun rising, white seagulls flying. It was a masterpiece.

Mr. Matamori exchanged excited words with his companions. "We would like to see now where the safety bags will be produced."

The other men, Mr. Tanaka and Mr. Aniko, nodded and followed as Ashley showed them the way.

The machines were older but in very good condition, as David Baxter explained while they watched several workers. They would be allotting more space if Bannister got the Tagami contract and hired new workers.

The two men nodded solemnly as Matamori explained David's words rapidly. Everyone smiled and Ashley felt herself relax. The contract they needed so badly seemed to be in the bag.

Between them, Ashley and David got everything on paper while Mr. Matamori went over their plan, changing it to align with what they had in mind.

David whistled. "That's a lot less than we figured."

"I know," Ashley agreed, looking at the final figures, biting her lip. Should she haggle? Bannister could still make money even if it wasn't what they'd planned.

The three men in their correct, dark suits watched her closely.

Gathering her tightly held belief in her family's company, Ashley wrote down another figure on the paper. She stepped back for the three Tagami reps to look at it. David glanced over their shoulders and nodded shortly.

Calculators whirred; the three dark heads stayed close together as they spoke in low tones. Mr. Tanaka pointed urgently at the figures on the page.

Finally, Mr. Matamori turned around to face her. He nodded curtly. "This is acceptable to us, Miss Bannister. We are ready to sign the contract with your company."

David Baxter shook his hand heartily, then shook hands with the other two men. All three men were laughing together, taking their turn shaking hands with Ashley as well.

"I got you a table at Franklin's Cove," Frances told Ashley, approaching her carefully as the group all laughed and talked at once. "Is everything all right?"

"Just fine," Ashley replied evenly. "Could you have those contracts ready to sign with the figures on the table when we get back from lunch?"

"We got it?" She smiled. "I can have those ready right away."

"Thanks," Ashley answered. "We should be back in a couple of hours."

David declined to leave the plant with them for lunch, saying he had too much work to finish. The three Tagami reps nodded in understanding and respect for the manager, shaking his hand again, then accompanying Ashley to the parking lot.

Mr. Matamori sat in the front seat of the car with Ashley driving while the other two sat in back. They exchanged remarks as she drove through the quiet streets, exclaiming at the rows of neat white houses and perfect green lawns.

They reached the center of town that consisted of tiny stores that had been there since the turn of the century. A new school and a spired courthouse made up the rest of downtown Martinsville. Traffic was being directed by a uniformed policeman around the corner from the square.

"Is there a problem?" Ashley asked as she passed him.

"New art thing going at the courthouse." He waved her past him.

With her visitors nearly hanging from the windows to see what was going on, Ashley parked the car and suggested they watch the event.

They were out of the car as soon as it stopped. Ashley walked slowly behind them as they quickly disappeared into the crowd on the street.

The sun was shining, warm on her head. She had a new contract in her pocket. Life was good for the mo-

ment. She stood off to the side, watching as they lowered a huge bronze statue of a hawk.

"You look like the cat who swallowed the cream,"
Trey remarked, from her side.

Ashley used her hand to shade her eyes from the
sun as she looked up into his face. She shivered at his
nearness. "Trey," she remarked as though she hadn't
been thinking about him all morning. "What brings
you out into the sunshine?"

"I never miss an unveiling," he replied with his
crooked smile intact. "What about you?"

"I'm taking some clients to lunch." She looked
through the group around her but saw no sign of the
Tagami reps. "They seem to be more interested in the
sights."

"You mean they prefer a statue to you?" he asked
with amazement in his clear voice.

Ashley looked up at him again just to see if he were
laughing at her. He swept his morning-gray eyes over
her and she immediately felt self-conscious. She
wished she'd had time to get her hair done. Her
straight white skirt felt too tight and she knew her face
was the same rose color as her silk blouse.

She straightened her shoulders. "I should look for
my guests."

"I suppose you should," he sympathized. "New
contract?"

"Yes," she acknowledged.

"If you're looking for the three men in the dark

business suits who look like triplets, I think they're over there.'' He pointed. ''Right at the front.''

When she still didn't see them, he used one hand to bring her in front of him, lowering his darker head beside her own light one to guide her gaze.

''You don't trust me, do you?'' he asked, his voice deceptively soft, close to her ear.

''Not at all.'' She stepped away from him and his hand dropped from her arm.

''Good.'' He nodded. ''That makes everything so much easier.''

She glared at him. ''Most people like to be trusted.''

''I'm not most people.'' He looked her over thoroughly in the clear sunlight. ''You don't look like you suffered any from last night's experience.''

''I've been kissed before,'' she told him defensively, her heart beating a wild tattoo against her chest.

He smiled and narrowed his eyes on her face. ''I meant your fall down the hill.''

''Oh. I'm fine,'' she replied, feeling like a silly schoolgirl. ''How about you?''

''I survived,'' he answered easily, putting his hands in his pockets to keep from touching her. ''I've been kissed before, too.''

''You are a wicked man, Trey Harris. I think I'm lucky you decided *not* to help me.''

''I think you could be right,'' he agreed pleasantly. ''For both our sakes.''

Chapter Three

It wasn't hard to find the old farm Trey Harris had been converting to his own use since he'd moved back to Martinsville. Ashley drove down the road from it and parked for a while, trying to build up her courage to approach him.

She headed back up the road, passing the long drive once more while she argued with all the voices in her head. It was getting late, she told herself. If she was going up that drive, she had better do it. It wasn't going to get any easier and it couldn't wait.

After the Tagami contract and the fiasco with Trey, she had decided to give up on asking for help. That is, until her lawyer had called her that morning with the ugly rumor that a competitor was about to buy up a large block of stock and take them over. She worried about it all day, then despite her better judgment, she started out for Trey's farm. She wasn't sure what she hoped to gain but she had to do something.

She negotiated the twisting drive in her green Saturn, marveling at the statues that lined the edges. A whole family of rabbits sat near a hollow stump. Two shy deer were watching her from a copse of maple trees. A dozen satyrs capered in the meadow among the golden-yellow honeysuckle and the wild pink roses. Their faces were a study in playful leering.

She knew they were his work. Just as the hawk in front of the town hall had been his work. Trey Harris was a man of energy and passion. Ashley had felt the will that drove him when she'd first encountered his eyes across the diner. She'd felt it in his arms when he'd kissed her, although she was trying to steer clear of those thoughts. She was there to talk business.

The house was white, an ordinary old farmhouse like so many that dotted the countryside. A wide porch ran the length of the outside. A few outbuildings and an old red barn were in the yard.

Two golden retrievers ran out of the barn to greet her, barking and wagging their plumed tails. A black-and-white cat proudly paraded her five kittens past her to the porch.

A massive bronze statue of a dragon kept guard, wings unfurled, on the ground near the front stairs.

''He's chained,'' Trey assured her as he followed the dogs out of the barn.

Ashley looked and there was a wide bronze chain that encircled the dragon's neck and was anchored in the ground. The whole thing was easily ten feet tall and incredibly intimidating.

"I've never seen anything like it," she told him in awe, appreciating the fine detail.

"I'm not sure with you, Ashley," he quipped. "Is that good or bad?"

"I'm sure you don't need me to tell you that you're a very good artist," she told him a little caustically.

"I'll take that as a compliment." His eyes roamed restlessly over her. "I was about to have some lemonade. Would you like some?"

It was as good a start as she could have hoped for and she grabbed it. "That sounds great."

"How was your lunch?" he wondered as she followed him up to the door.

"It went very well," she replied politely, going into the house as he held the screen door open. "They were very impressed with your statue."

"Thanks." He guided her toward the kitchen. "My great-grandfather helped build that town hall. I dedicated it to him."

"Is that what made you come back after so long?" she asked, discounting Frances's notion that he had been sent there for them.

He motioned with an expressive hand for her to take a stool at the wide bar. "It was my sister. She still lives here with her husband and their son. They're the only family I have left."

Ashley looked around the huge kitchen while he filled two glasses with ice and lemonade. It was modern, well equipped, and immaculate. Acres of white cabinet top gleamed under the bright lights. The floor was gray slate. The walls looked like the original wood.

It looked like him, she decided. Lean, artistic, and a little arrogant. There was none of the clutter she would have expected in an artist's home. None of the pictures or the bric-a-brac that her mother loved so much.

"I spent the last five years in New York. I came back for my mother's funeral last year and I realized that I had missed Martinsville . . . and even more important, that I had missed my sister Judy."

Ashley nodded as she took the glass of lemonade from him. "Frances told me about your mother. They went to school together, you know. I'm sorry you lost her."

He looked up at her sharply. "Ashley, why are you here?"

She sipped her lemonade, hoping he wouldn't see her hands trembling. "There's a rumor about a stock buyout."

"Have you ever been to New York?" he asked, changing the subject abruptly as he took a stool opposite her at the bar.

"No." She glanced away from his close scrutiny, uncomfortably aware of him. He looked as though he had just showered. His hair was damp and loose on his shoulders and his shirt was open at the throat. He looked relaxed, for once. Her words seemed to have no effect on him.

"It was strange being there after growing up in Martinsville. Now it seems strange to be here again."

Ashley smiled. "It must have been a big leap of faith for you to come back again."

Trey's eyes were hard when she looked back at him. He looked away. It would have been much easier if he hadn't gone to sleep thinking about her. It would have been even easier if he had never held her in his arms or kissed her.

He slipped his lemonade that was suddenly too sour on his tongue. "There wasn't any faith involved in it, Ashley. I lost that ten years ago." He was trying to put her in proper perspective. She was Parish Bannister's daughter. He couldn't possibly be attracted to her.

"I suppose love overcomes doubts like those," she faltered, knowing from his tone of voice that she had lost. She wished she could get up and walk out.

"In your case, I suppose that's true," he concluded thoughtfully. "I'd heard your father turned the company over to you. I haven't heard why you didn't marry Johnny."

Her fine brows arched delicately. "You've been listening to the Ashley Bannister story."

"It's not hard to find someone around here who knows it," he explained. "And they all want to talk about it."

"Small towns," she replied, embarrassed and uneasy. He'd been asking questions about her.

"Your father was very sure that Johnny could rejuvenate his company. He must have been very disappointed." He didn't look at her as he was speaking, and his voice was carefully blank. Ashley felt cold and uncomfortable.

"It's old news anyway," she breezed ahead, taking the opening. "You know why I'm here." She flashed him a winning smile.

He poured them both another glass of lemonade. "I know your shoe size, Ashley. I know your engagement didn't work and Johnny bailed on your father. But you'll have to fill in the rest. How do you think I could help you?"

"I thought I was very clear about it." She stiffened, clutching her glass like a lifeline. "I want you to help the company get back on its feet. You know things about management, particularly in Bannister's field, that could save us."

His eyes took on the look of cold stone. "Why would you think I would help you save Parish Bannister's company?"

"I told you, I'd pay you—"

"And I told you there isn't enough money in the world. Nothing would suit me better than to see his company go down the drain."

They faced each other across the bar, eyes locked on each other's faces. Ashley's face felt hot with humiliation.

"Then I guess there's nothing more to say." She stood up from her stool with great dignity and gave him a look that she felt sure would freeze molten lava. "I don't know if I can make Bannister work without you, but I won't beg."

He stared at that proud face, seeing a trace of her father in her determined features. There was a sheen of tears in her eyes and a slight quiver to her lips that caught him off guard. He strengthened his resolve. He couldn't, he wouldn't, feel sorry for her.

Ashley held herself rigidly together in the face of his stony rejection. "My father was wrong but he paid for his mistake. He was never the same about the business after you were gone and Johnny left me. Does that make you feel better? Knowing that his life was miserable?"

"You're like your father after all," he told her, his eyes glittering. "You may look like an angel but you think like him."

"Will this settle your score with my father?" she demanded. "Will three hundred other people losing their jobs make you feel better?"

He looked away from her, shaking his head. "Go home, Ashley. Your problems don't mean anything to me."

"That doesn't surprise me," she retorted, knowing that she had nothing to lose. "Everyone thought that you'd gone on with your life. They were wrong, weren't they? Well, now maybe you can finally let it go."

"The world isn't made of white picket fences and

pretty flowers. Nobody gets something for nothing. Grow up.''

She bit her lip. ''I have ten thousand dollars in a trust fund.''

He stared at her in disbelief. ''I don't want your money.''

''What do you want?''

It only took a step to bring her against him and stop the words with his mouth on hers. It was only a heartbeat that she lay quiescent in his arms, her mind in turmoil while her heart reacted as though they had been in love for years.

He released her as quickly. ''Leave me alone, Ashley.''

Ashley stared at him, reeling from the emotional impact. She tried to force herself to find something else to say but her tongue wouldn't move. Without another word, she stormed from his house and slammed the door behind her.

Trey heard the sound of her tires skidding down the drive before he relaxed his stance. He was a fool. He'd broken his own rule of survival for the last ten years. He'd gotten involved. She made him remember the past that he'd promised himself he would never think through again. All the pain and anger he'd felt ten years before came to life again when she spoke to him. Then she kissed him and somehow it had all threatened to go away with the taste of summer on her pretty pink lips. He wasn't sure how he felt about giving up the past. He didn't want to feel anything for Ashley Bannister.

He spent the night working on a new piece of work that he had promised to a man in New Mexico. It was detailed and exacting and he was able to push everything else out of his mind. Yet in the morning, he saw her eyes again, felt the rigid control she'd exercised over herself to keep from falling apart.

He stared at his tired reflection in the bathroom mirror, wondering if he could let those memories go. Then he collapsed on his bed, sleeping dreamlessly.

Pushing himself out the door a few days later, determined not to think about Ashley Bannister again in his life, he drove to the hospital.

It was a glorious summer day. There was so much life going on around him that he felt as though he could stand outside his door and breathe it all without getting enough.

The sound of the bees and the scent of the wildflowers—those were the things he had missed living in the city. Colts ran in the green fields with their mothers. A hawk flew overhead. Life here was rich with texture and color.

He'd called the hospital that morning. Bill Raymond's condition had been upgraded that day from critical to stable. He was breathing on his own but he hadn't shown any signs of recognizing anyone, and there was some paralysis.

Trey spoke with Bill's wife and daughter when he

arrived, then looked up when someone called his name.

"Is that you, young Harris?"

Clement Johnson, nearly seventy, had worked at Bannister for over forty years. He'd been there long enough to call Parish Bannister a fool when he'd let Trey go.

"Clement!" Trey shook his hand. "You aren't still working?"

"I'm afraid so." The older man laughed, a wheezing sound in his barrel chest. "Got nothing better to do."

Two other men, Joe Hardin and Zeke Carriker, shook Trey's hand as well. They had all worked at the Bannister plant for years.

"So," Zeke was the first to speak up, "are you gonna help us or what?"

Trey glanced at the man. He was at least sixty, only about five feet tall, and weighed less than most teenagers. Yet he was a force to be reckoned with when it came time to get something done.

"I don't think there's anything I can do," Trey answered, not quite honestly.

"There might be plenty," Clement spoke steadily. "But you're still ticked off by what old Parish did ten years ago. Aren't you?"

Uncomfortably, Trey had to acknowledge that what he said was true. "I don't want to get involved again."

"What Parish did was rotten," Clement agreed. "The new one, Miss Ashley, she's a different person than her daddy. She wouldn't do you wrong like he did for that sneaky little Thompson boy.''

''I don't think—''

''And if she did—'' Zeke came up close to him, his left eye winking ''—you could cut her off fast this time. Take care of yourself first. Know what I mean?''

Trey heard the man's words echo in his head all the way back to the farm.

He wasn't sure when he'd decided that he was going to get involved. If he were honest, it might have been when he'd realized that he admired Ashley's courage in facing him.

Or it had happened when he had seen those men's lined and worn faces. He knew those faces. Old Zeke had been the crossing guard after school when he was a boy. Those men and women he had worked with at the plant were neighbors. They had brought his mother applesauce cake and sweet potato pie when his father had died.

Their jobs were part of the three hundred Ashley had urged him to consider when he'd told her he wouldn't help. Their families were depending on her for their paychecks.

Whatever the reason, he fought with himself most of another night and ended up losing. Early the next morning, a full day's beard on his face, his clothes rumpled and eyes reddened from working through the night, he presented himself at Ashley's office.

Ashley looked up from her files, seated behind the

huge old desk. Her eyes followed up from his muscled chest beneath the rough gray shirt he wore to his obstinate chin and wintry eyes.

"Is there somewhere we can talk?"

"Pardon me?" Ashley swallowed hard and tried to gather her wits.

"I'm on my way to the hospital," Frances said cheerfully, getting up quickly from her desk.

"Frances, I—" Ashley tried to detain her.

"It's good to see you again, Trey," Frances acknowledged.

"Thanks." Trey nodded. "You, too."

When the door had closed behind her, Ashley waited, holding her hands together tightly to keep him from seeing how nervous he made her. What was he doing? Hadn't he made his position clear?

"I've thought your problem over carefully, Ashley, and I have a temporary solution that you probably won't like."

"Oh?" she wondered, trying not to be resentful of his command of the situation. "I thought you weren't interested in my problems."

"I didn't think there was any time to waste," he continued, ignoring her remark. "There's only one way this would work to benefit the company right now. You would have to hire me as a management consultant and let everyone know who I am and what we're doing."

"I see." That didn't sound so bad to her, and in

fact, it was what she had in mind. Except the part about telling everyone else.

"It gets harder," he cautioned. "From the beginning, you and I have to have an understanding that I'm going to do what's best for the company. You have to trust me and you have to give me complete authority to do whatever needs to be done."

"It is my company, Trey," she replied coolly. "While I would appreciate any suggestion—"

"Then you're on your own," he cut in roughly. "The only way this works is straight down the middle."

"Why? What difference could it possibly make?" she demanded angrily.

He put his hands on the cluttered desktop, bringing himself closer to her eye level. "It would raise confidence in your stockholders. They wouldn't be in such a hurry to sell. They'd want to wait and see what was going to happen. A lot of people still remember what I did here ten years ago."

"It sounds like some sort of ego trip to me," she scoffed, folding her arms protectively across her chest.

"You were the one who approached me," he reminded her.

"And you turned me down, remember? What made you go through this change of heart?"

"Because I realized that you were right," he admitted, running a careless hand through his long hair. "This isn't about you or your father. It's about Zeke Carriker and Frances and Clement Johnson."

She stared at him. "How do I know that I can trust you?"

"I'm good for two things that you need right now, Ashley."

"And those are?"

"A diversion to throw off Marshall and Seymour. While they're waiting to see what's going to happen, they won't be trying to bid on your contracts. After all, if they bid too fast, you might undercut them."

"What do you mean?" she asked doubtfully. "They've found new suppliers and machinery that cuts their prices. We can't possibly hope to match them."

"That's the second thing. I can play their game, Ashley. You can't. You're not ruthless enough."

Ashley looked at him, wishing she could see past the bright eyes and the grim smile to the man beneath. Frances had said she had the gift from her grandfather. She hoped her assistant was right or he would be turning in his grave.

"All right," she decided finally, despite her damaged pride. "We'll try it your way."

"I want a contract, Ashley." He shook his head as she started to speak. "With specifics just as we've discussed."

"And what do you want for this?" She edged further over the precipice, throwing her caution to the wind.

"Nothing, if it doesn't work," he answered squarely. "A percentage of the profits if it does."

"How much?" she queried.

"Thirty percent for one year following the turnaround."

"That's too much," she replied curtly. "Ten percent for the year and company stock at the going rate before your plan."

He scrutinized her face. Its smooth contours gave away nothing.

"Get me the contract before the weekend." He nodded and put out his hand. "I think we can pull it off."

Ashley put her hand into his and felt his long fingers close around hers. There was a jolt of electricity between them, then a silky wash of energy began to seep up her wrist.

"Done," she said briskly. "Welcome to Bannister Manufacturing, Mr. Harris."

"I'm sure I'll enjoy working with you, Ms. Bannister," he answered smoothly, not releasing her hand.

Ashley wished she could feel that confident. She'd just been telling herself that she was lucky he had turned her down. That working with him would have been impossible. That his touch left her restless and dazed. Why had he changed his mind? Could she let him in to save her company without ruining her life?

Ashley sent out the papers by messenger to Trey's farm and paced the floor in her bedroom the rest of the night. It was too late to wonder if what she'd done was right. But she could certainly worry about the consequences.

The next day was a busy Friday. It was over before

she realized that she hadn't heard from him or seen him.

Perversely, she was angry at first, wondering if his words had merely been a smokescreen. Wasn't he the one who made it sound imperative to go at it as quickly as possible? She refused to think about how she had listened attentively for the sound of his voice all day. Or that she had been disappointed when she hadn't seen him walk around a corner toward her.

''Tough day,'' David said as they were leaving the plant together.

''Monday's going to be worse,'' she assured him with a frown.

''Ashley,'' Frances greeted her from the office. ''I got those letters out just a few minutes ago.''

''Letters?'' Ashley wondered as David waved good night and walked by her into the parking lot.

''The letters for the stockholders Trey asked me to get out ASAP.'' Frances beamed. ''They'll be in the morning mail. The editor at the Gazette assured me that the notice about Trey Harris coming back to work here would be in Sunday's paper.''

''Great!'' Ashley grunted, not really sure what re-percussions there would be when everyone opened those letters. Why had he avoided her? Not that it wasn't for the best. She really didn't want to see him. They always either fought . . . or kissed.

The headache she used as an excuse not to go out to dinner with a friend that night was real enough. She ate a little fresh corn soup in her room while the sounds of her mother's bridge group filtered upstairs.

Sitting in the middle of her bed, trade magazines around her, Atlanta Braves short pajamas on, she plaited her still-damp hair back away from her face.

The evening was getting late but the light still held, a little fuzzy, on the rosebushes and the emerald green of the freshly mowed lawn.

The sky was a dull gray that came with heat and pollution. The air-conditioning inside the big house was on full force to keep out the humidity and the stifling late-June weather.

Ashley had barely finished her hair when there was a knock on the door. Thinking Mandy, her mother's housekeeper, had come to badger her about not eating again, she got up and went to take the empty soup bowl to the door.

"It was really good but I couldn't eat another . . ." Her voice trailed off when she saw who was at the door.

Trey Harris, in sleek black tuxedo and crisp white shirt, smiled and looked down at the empty bowl.

"Looks good," he determined, putting his finger in the bowl then sticking it into his mouth. "You're right. I'm convinced."

She followed the progress of his finger into his mouth before she realized that she was watching him. "What are you doing here?"

"I have some papers I want you to look at before

Monday.'' His gaze went lazily down her bare legs. ''Maybe now is a bad time?''

She put the bowl down carelessly on the side table. ''Surely they could have waited until Monday morning?''

''I won't be in until late Monday,'' he advised. ''But if this is a problem . . . ?''

''All right.'' She gave in, her hand still on the door. ''I'll be down in a minute.''

''I'll wait.''

She closed the door and pulled on an old robe that had seen its better days when she was about sixteen.

How often had she promised herself a new one? Mostly when she embarrassed herself, getting the paper in the driveway or answering the door. Those were the times she wished she had thrown the thing away.

Knowing she was wearing it to meet with a business partner who was wearing a tux didn't help her attitude. The fact that it was Trey made it worse.

He was waiting in the turn of the stairs, leaning negligently against the rail.

Ashley paused and looked down at him. He was an incredibly handsome man with his out-of-fashion long, dark hair and his icy gray eyes. Those eyes hadn't been cold just then when he'd looked at her. In fact, she hadn't realized that gray could catch fire.

She wondered, briefly, where he was going that night. Not that it mattered. She was just curious. Of course, there would be a woman in his life.

''Come in here.'' She brushed by him as she

stepped off the bottom step. A loud shout of laughter came from behind the closed dining room door. "My mother's bridge game is a little loud tonight."

"Nice house," he observed, following her into the library. "Very . . . *Gone with the Wind.*"

"Thanks." She frowned, pushing a stray piece of hair back from her scrubbed face. "What's the problem?"

"I didn't mean to make you uncomfortable," he told her earnestly. "I really didn't expect you to be here. I was going to leave the papers."

"It's all right," she lied. "I'm not uncomfortable."

"I met your lawyer at a cocktail party earlier," he remarked, looking at the collection of swords above the hearth. "You didn't tell him yet."

She lifted her chin. "I'm was going to tell him Monday. I wanted to talk to him in person."

"Bringing in an outsider is always hard," he observed candidly. "You're afraid of his reaction."

"He won't be any different when he finds out," she assured him. "He'll back my decision."

Trey glanced at her curiously but didn't pursue the subject. "Anyway, these papers are some things you should look over as soon as possible. There are some changes I'm going to see made right away. And I wanted to talk to you about the balloon rally next weekend."

She looked up at him defensively before she took the papers. "What about it?"

"It's held every year for the stockholders, employees, families. Sort of a barbecue and goodwill thing. I went once myself.''

''And?'' she said, feeling as though something were closing in around her.

''I want to be there,'' he proposed. ''It would give you an opportunity to introduce me around, let me talk to some of the stockholders. There'll probably be a lot of people I already know.''

''It's next weekend. Everything's all planned.'' She started to doubt the wisdom of inviting him to the balloon rally. ''I don't know—''

''Frances thought it was a good idea,'' he quipped smartly. ''Any reason I shouldn't be there?''

A hundred reasons popped into her mind but she backed down. ''No, not really. I guess after everyone gets the letters, it won't matter.''

''Ashley, you're not having second thoughts?''

''Well—''

''Too bad.'' He ended whatever she'd been about to say. ''I'm here until we can get this together. Trust me, it's going to work out.''

She eyed him narrowly. ''I thought you said it was better that I didn't trust you.''

''That was before I worked for you.'' He smiled and put the papers he'd held into her hands, his fingers sliding lazily across her own. ''I'm your man, boss.''

Ashley watched that straight back and those broad shoulders as he walked away from her. There was a definite arrogance to the way he held his head. A noticeable scar at the corner of his mouth might have been where someone had taken his attitude the wrong way. She could imagine that happening to him.

She could even imagine helping put another one on the other side. The man certainly brought out strong emotions.

Chapter Four

Ashley slammed into the red brick building Monday morning with the force of a hurricane.

"Where is he?" she demanded, looking as though Frances were hiding him in her lemon-yellow skirt.

"He won't be in until three," Frances replied stoically, not batting an eyelash at Ashley's anger. Trey had warned her that there might be fireworks.

"When he does come in, make sure he knows I want to see him," she demanded, a little deflated that she had to wait.

The man was an inhuman monster! His ideas of cost reduction and control were like something from the Middle Ages!

She had arranged to meet with her lawyer, Rusty Lee, for lunch that day to explain the logistics of Trey being there. Her biggest stockholder, her mother, would be there as well. Between them, she usually felt like she was in a shredder.

Work kept her from worrying too much. There was so much to be done and not a lot of time to do it. Their new contract called for them to start production the following week and they were still short ten machines for the Tagami air bag job.

Losing track of the time, Ashley was surprised to see Rusty at her side long before it seemed like lunch. She and Rusty had gone to school together. They dated irregularly. Everyone expected them to get married someday.

"Honey!" Rusty tried to get her attention through the noise in the factory.

"I have to change," she told him loudly. "I won't be a minute."

"Take your time, Ashley," Margaret Bannister, carefully garbed in green silk, told her daughter. "Rusty and I can wait for this explanation."

Ashley watched her mother take Rusty's arm, their heads bent close together, as they walked out to the car together.

"Frances, I hope we were right," she told her assistant through tightly clenched teeth.

"What's up?" Frances followed her into the cubbyhole she used for a storage room.

"It looks as though I'll be taking Rusty and Mother out for lunch and an explanation," she told her grimly, pulling open her workout bag and shaking out her blue dress, scrounging for her pantyhose.

There was a ventilation pipe that formed a natural screen at the side of the office. Ashley had used the space behind it to change clothes since she was a child. She ducked behind it and stripped off her jeans and work shirt.

"I wanted to have a chance to thrash your hero before I had to defend him," she told her assistant.

"You just have to stand up for what you've done, Ashley," Frances told her firmly.

"Would you mind going out to lunch with us and explaining that?" Ashley wondered, pulling her dress on over her head.

"Not at all," Trey answered simply.

"You!" Ashley hit her head and dropped her shoes. They rolled under the ventilation pipe. She hastily pulled up the zipper on her dress.

He picked up her white shoes and handed them to her under the vent pipe. Now she saw that from where he stood, the pipe ran straight up. She felt reasonably sure that he hadn't seen her changing clothes.

"Sorry, I didn't mean to startle you. Get the whips and chains," he told her, settling back in a folding chair.

"I wish I had time for that now," she warned him, slipping her feet into her shoes. She slid from behind the vent, feeling a little ridiculous.

"I'd love to tell you what I think of those cuts you gave me Saturday night." She stuffed her work clothes into the bag, snagging her finger on the zipper and wincing.

"Is that all?" he asked calmly. He stretched up and closed the hook at the top of her dress while she adjusted her belt.

"You knew that I wouldn't want those changes made," she continued to protest as she brushed her hair in the sliver of mirror on the wall. She dropped her lip gloss and he picked it up, handing it to her wordlessly.

Ashley looked at him as his fingers touched her own. He wore a white shirt and khaki pants, a Bannister cap pulled down low on his head so that she had to look up into his eyes.

"You knew when you hired me that some of the things I did were going to be that way," he replied finally. "Not everything can be the way you want it. Those changes will help save the company."

"Not that Mother and Rusty are concerned about the changes you want to make," she answered hotly, stepping away from him. "They're concerned about you."

"More reason to take me with you. I'm great moral support."

"They won't want to hear about the changes, Trey."

"Of course they will! The changes I've made will affect them both as shareholders."

"Changes you've *made?*"

"Read my contract, Ashley," he reminded her bluntly. "I have the power to effect changes in certain areas."

"But I didn't think you'd do anything without my final approval!"

He looked at her closely, no sign of what he was thinking in his face. "You have a smudge on your cheek," he said finally. "I'm going with you."

Ashley scrubbed at the mark with a tissue. Anger fueled her as she set out from the office, passing David as she went through the plant.

"Don't envy you that group," he said, shaking his head and setting his cap back. "But those are some mighty fine machines."

"What?" she asked, almost missing what he'd said as she was trying to get out the door.

"The machines Trey brought back from the old Cane place that went under last year. They are beauties!"

Margaret Bannister was laughing with Trey in the backseat of Ashley's Saturn. The air-conditioning was running so cold that the windows were beginning to frost from the inside. Frost had also already formed on Rusty's face in the front seat and there didn't seem to be any sign of a thaw.

Trey glanced up at her as she opened the car door and Ashley felt it was obvious what he was thinking. Divide and conquer.

"Sorry it took so long." She smiled and got behind the wheel. "How about Eddie's for lunch?"

"That sounds fine to me," her mother gushed. "What about you, Trey?"

"I've never been there but I'm always looking for new places."

"I've always hated their sandwiches," Rusty told them before anyone could ask.

"But you like their salads," Ashley reminded him. "And they won't be very crowded."

The trip went the same way. Margaret and Trey laughing together in the backseat. Rusty refusing to look at, or speak to Ashley, as she drove through town.

"So that's your work." Margaret pointed out the hawk as they passed the courthouse. "I'd love to have a smaller one for the yard."

"I have a satyr that would love to live with you," Trey suggested. "He's a little more . . . romantic . . . than the hawk."

Ashley gritted her teeth and put her foot down a little harder on the gas pedal.

Eddie's wasn't crowded, as Ashley had predicted, and the smell of their famous onion rings filled the place.

"Four for lunch," Rusty unwound enough to tell the host when he arrived to seat them. "Why didn't you tell me?" he whispered to Ashley, catching her arm to hold her back from the other two as they followed the waiter.

"There wasn't time," she answered, somewhat truthfully. "I was going to tell you today."

"After the letters went out?" he demanded in a hiss.

"I did what was necessary."

"Without even consulting me?" he asked her harshly. "I thought we were closer."

"One has nothing to do with the other," she finished.

"Trust, Ashley." He sniffed, sitting beside her at the table. "Trust."

Trey watched the two of them from the corner of his eye. Was there something going on between them that he hadn't heard about?

Margaret excused herself to the ladies' room. Rusty gave Ashley a long look, then went to the salad bar.

"Relax," Trey whispered, his lips almost grazing her ear.

Ashley felt his dark head brush by her own, his hand on her shoulder for reassurance.

"I suppose you're an old hand at this, too?" she wondered, shivering. She looked at her plate instead of his face. She had tried really hard to forget the kisses they'd shared on those other occasions. When he wasn't so close, it was much easier.

"Ashley, honey," he mimicked Rusty's Southern drawl, "I've schmoozed with the best of them."

"I'm sure you have." She laughed despite herself, looking at his face quickly. Her eyes caught on something in his gaze that wouldn't let her look away and she felt the blood rush to her face. For an instant, they were alone again and his lips were so close. . . .

"You bet." Trey moved back suddenly, recalling where they were and what they were doing. He broke a bread stick between his fingers.

Ashley stared at those long, tapering hands. "How did you start sculpting?"

"What?"

She could see that her question had taken him by surprise. "Surely someone must have asked you that question before?" she defended. "I mean, being a famous artist." She was delighted to see him disconcerted for once. A small, reckless smile formed on her face.

He looked at the bread stick then at his hands before he finally returned his gaze to her. There was no mistaking the purely feminine look of triumph on Ashley's face.

"Why, Ashley, are you flirting with me?" He eyed her speculatively. "I thought you were such a nice Southern lady."

"In other words," she theorized, "you don't encounter many people asking you that question living in Martinsville. You keep to yourself and sidestep the private stuff."

"You could say that." He nodded, a gleam in his light gaze that caressed her face. He couldn't quite bring himself to move all the way across the table from her. "Actually, I wouldn't mind if you were flirting with me, Ashley."

"I was not flirting." She cleared her throat. "Really. What made you start sculpting? It seems like a strange thing for a man like you."

"A man like me." He played with the words on his

lips. "That seems an unfair statement since you don't know anything about me."

"I know that you went to college for business management and ended up sculpting," she qualified, trying to avoid watching him as he spoke.

"You don't want to know what came between, Ashley," he promised her.

"My father?" she demanded fiercely.

He looked back at her, not able to look away. She was so close that he could smell her perfume, see a tiny imperfection in her delicately blushed cheek. It was impossible for him to believe that he could be attracted to Parish Bannister's daughter. But the proof was sitting so close beside him that it was all he could do not to touch her.

"You know, I think they water down this salad dressing." Rusty joined them with a plate in each hand, not noticing that they were startled at his arrival.

"It's just an excuse for you to put more on," Margaret told him as she slid in next to Trey.

"So, down to business." Ashley pushed them all forward as Margaret's food arrived.

She hoped her voice didn't sound as breathless as she felt inside. She could feel Trey sitting there beside her like a palpable heat source, raising her temperature and her blood pressure until it was nearly unbearable. "I've hired Trey to be our management consultant."

"An excellent choice," Margaret approved. "I'm sure he'll be very creative."

"I don't think you should have done this without our knowledge," Rusty told her briefly.

"I don't consult you each time I make a decision, Rusty," Ashley told him. "Neither of you know what contracts we get or how the plant runs except for the letter you get quarterly."

"I'm not interested in the plant," Margaret agreed, taking Trey's arm. "You know this thing killed your father. And if Rusty is smart, he'll get you out of this before it happens to you."

"I told her she should sell the plant and get married," Rusty defended himself.

"Never mind." Ashley shook her head. "This isn't personal. It's business. I think Trey has some good ideas for the company that will help us get through for a while."

"Let me share a few of those ideas with you, Rusty, Margaret, and let's see what you think," Trey picked up the conversation.

Lunch was necessarily brief since Ashley had to get back to the plant. It hadn't been as bad as she'd expected, although Rusty couldn't be won over to the idea of Trey doing anything with Bannister.

Margaret, on the other hand, seemed ready to give him whatever he needed. Ashley knew she hadn't heard all of it from her mother but she felt the first round had gone well.

"I'll see you this weekend then, Trey," Margaret told him when they were getting out of the car at the plant.

"I'll be there," he answered, taking her beautifully manicured hand in his own.

"Wonderful," Rusty breathed, slamming his car door and taking off out of the parking lot without a word to Ashley.

"Well?" Trey asked Ashley after the other two had left.

"Well what?" she demanded when he'd caught up with her.

"How do you think it went?"

"I don't know." She shuddered and walked into the building. The cool air was a relief after the hot sun glaring off the pavement. And that reminded her of something.

"Frances," she instructed as she retrieved her tote bag from her desk, "we need to make an appointment for next week for the pavement in the parking lot."

Frances looked behind Ashley at Trey and Ashley knew she was in trouble.

"We're not going to do that right now," Trey told her.

"But we do that every year at this time," she told him angrily.

"Part of that money went for the new machines," he explained patiently.

Ashley came full circle to face him. "Where did the rest of the money come from for the machines?"

"Here and there." He shrugged. "And an exchange for some things that we have that we don't need."

"And how did you know we didn't need them?"

"David and Zeke. Frances made me a list of everything in the plant. I went from there."

"By the way, Ashley, David has been up here three times looking for you," Frances chimed in, putting an end to the discussion.

Frustrated, not used to being manipulated and worked around, Ashley slammed out of the office.

"She's always been very high spirited," Francis smiled and told him. "I have some messages for you as well, Trey."

"I'll take them in the other office," he told her. "Thanks. And Frances?"

"Hmm?" she asked.

"Some of that money is for the new computer system. It'll be here the end of the week. Think we can keep it away from Ashley until it's installed?"

"I'll think of something," she promised.

"You're a jewel," he added, leaving her with the charm of his smile.

"I know," she agreed, feeling a flutter in her heart.

The rest of the week was long and frustrating. Staying away from the office, letting Frances start hiring the new workers, Ashley helped David in the plant, training workers to use the new equipment.

In the meantime, several big balloons were being finished for the balloon rally that weekend. Their delivery driver called in with the bad news that the truck was down a day before delivery was due.

Since it was the Fourth of July, everyone was moving everything, everywhere. Parades, carnivals, air shows. Frances was on the phone all day but couldn't come up with another truck or another driver.

Ashley, already dirty from working on a few of the machines they were trying to get set up for production the next week, called Rusty and asked him to bring his truck.

"I'll take it up to Lexington," she told Frances, wiping her hands on a gray towel.

"I can do that, Ashley," David offered. It was bad enough that she was standing there with a black smudge on her face, wearing dirty jeans and a T-shirt. He respected Ashley but sometimes he thought she forgot who she was when it came to the company.

"I need you here to work on these machines," she told him bluntly. "I'm the only one who's really expendable here today."

Frances frowned her disapproval as well but they both knew what she said made sense. Besides, they knew she had been pushed as far as she was going to be pushed that week.

"I don't know nothing about it if your mother asks," Zeke denied, walking away.

Ashley had set up a small desk for herself in the plant manager's office after Frances had told her that they were going to be working on the ventilation in the office for the next week.

"It's the only reasonable thing to do," Ashley told them, wiping dirt from her face on the red bandanna she'd had on her hair. "Unless my mother wants to come and haul this up there herself."

"You know best," David muttered darkly.

"Then we'll load up when Rusty gets here. I'll take it up there, then meet you for the rally," she decided.

David threw up his hands and walked away.

Ashley went back to her makeshift desk, sitting on it while she looked over the setup on the new sewing machines.

"Busy?" Trey asked.

"Not right now." She put down the schematics. "The machines are all in and almost set up for next week. I don't know how you got them—"

"Nothing even vaguely illegal," he assured her briefly.

She eyed him narrowly. "Feeling guilty?"

"You could just say thanks and let it go," he suggested hopefully.

"Thanks," she replied.

"You're welcome. That wasn't so hard, was it?"

She stared into his gleaming eyes and smiled. "I'm not sure. I always feel like I just lost something when I do what you want me to do."

The smile on her face and the tilt of her pretty head made his hands itch to pull her to him, grease and all, and kiss her. He put his hands in his pockets to resist the impulse. It was best not to mix business with pleasure. It would have been best not to see her every day if he wanted to resist mixing business with pleasure. It didn't get easier.

"Rusty's here," Zeke called out from the doorway. "Just got that truck waxed, too."

"Excuse me." Ashley left Trey at the desk. "Is the balloon ready?" she asked, not encouraging the men around her.

"As ready as it can be to go in that thing," David answered with a smattering of laughter from a few other workers.

Ashley frowned at them, then walked out to meet Rusty. Most work stopped as they watched her from the cool interior of the building.

"Pompous idiot," David growled beneath his breath. "He's not good enough to clean her shoes."

Trey listened to a host of comments from the plant workers, wondering if Ashley knew how hot a topic her "romance" with Rusty Lee was for them.

"You look terrible." Rusty shook his head in disapproval. "Isn't there someone else that can do that stuff?"

"What stuff?" she demanded, wiping her face with her hand and leaving another faint streak.

"Work on those machines." He saw the frown line begin on her forehead but continued anyway. He would have his say. "Ashley, hire another mechanic or something! You're a mess!"

"Thanks," she acknowledged with a tired nod.

"I have to go," he told her. "Sorry, hon, but Mr. Weyrich finally decided to make out his last will and testament and I'm working with his lawyer to draw it up."

"That's all right. Thanks for bringing the truck

over.'' She handed him her car keys so that he could get back.

''Probably have to skip dinner tonight, too,'' he warned, walking to her car. ''No telling how many assets this man wants to distribute.''

''I'm taking the balloon up tonight anyway. I'll probably just spend the night up there. Coming up?''

''I'll be there,'' he answered and, conscious of the interested eyes watching them from the building, Rusty grabbed her up close to him and kissed her hard on the mouth.

There was a chorus of unmistakable gagging sounds and laughter from the plant.

''We should talk this weekend, Ashley. Seriously.'' Rusty's face mirrored surprise at the strength of her return kiss, but he kept his equilibrium. ''I'll see you tomorrow.''

With a quelling look at his unseen hecklers, Rusty started the Saturn and pulled out of the parking lot.

Ashley watched the car leave, releasing a pent-up breath of air. What had prompted such a thing from Rusty? A kiss in a parking lot, especially with an audience, was the equivalent of singing on stage for him. Any kiss, besides a glancing kiss on her cheek when they said good night, was unusual.

She had kissed him back with more enthusiasm than was necessary as well. It was knowing that Trey was watching from the building, a small voice whispered.

It was summer madness. She drowned out that small

voice. She didn't care what Trey thought of her relationship with Rusty.

"If everyone's done gawking." She turned to the small group that was gathered just within the shelter of the building. "I think we have a balloon to load up."

It took ten of them to load the balloon into the back of the pickup. Usually, Bannister balloons traveled in bigger trucks and the balloon didn't have to be pushed into such a small space. One tear in the fabric and the balloon had to be repaired. Not an image that any company liked to start with at the rally.

The gondola, the basket they would ride in, was a deep golden yellow. Years of use had deepened the patina of finish that protected it from the weather, but the handmade basket was sound.

Ashley helped tie down the black tarp over the bed of the truck then brushed the dust from her jeans. The gondola was hoisted up and held in place near the front of the truck bed with bungee cords.

"I'll leave the FAA papers on the dash," David told her. "Bobby'll meet you up there. He's got a new crew this year."

She nodded. "I'll be in Lexington before dark. Everything should be ready for tomorrow."

She changed into clean jeans and a blue button-up shirt after washing a little in the ladies' room. She would have liked to take a shower but there wasn't enough time to go home. She brushed her hair briskly then left it loose, planning on riding with her window open in the clear weather.

"Good time to finish up those computers," Frances told Trey as she passed him. "Ashley is going to Lexington and she won't be back until Sunday."

"Really?" He watched Ashley back the big blue truck out of the parking lot. She looked his way just for an instant. She couldn't see him, of course, in the dark shade of the plant. But the smile on her face etched itself on his mind.

"I think I can have the computer up in about an hour." He put his arm around Frances's shoulders as they walked back to the office. "How far did you say it is to Lexington?"

Chapter Five

Ashley drove out on the highway, passing larger motor homes and campers that were slowly leaving the city for the weekend. The roads weren't bad yet. She knew they would be in a few hours, when people started leaving for the weekend.

Rusty's truck drove well, even with the extra weight. He always kept it in perfect running order. His CDs were neatly stacked in their case and there was not a speck of dust on the faultless Carolina-blue paint.

Not that Ashley was finding fault. Rusty had been there for her as he had always been there when she needed him. When Johnny had left her, when her father had died. Rusty had been there to hold her hand and see her through it. He was a good man. Even though they didn't always agree. She knew, without being told, that he would do anything for her.

He had asked her to marry him once. At the time, she felt as though he made the offer because he felt sorry for her. He was honest, stable, dependable. His business did well. His family would never want for anything. Rusty was respected in Martinsville and he was content to be a big fish in the proverbial small pond. He had never married. Sometimes, they talked about getting married. So many people just assumed that they would marry one day.

Was that what he wanted to talk to her about over the weekend? If so, would she accept this time? Surely she wasn't still holding out for violins and sweaty palms. Surely she had learned her lesson that solid and dependable was better. She did care for him. They could have a sane, sympathetic relationship that would endure.

Aggressively, she put her foot down on the accelerator and passed a double trailer truck.

Would there always be that little part in her that wanted to be in love, really in love? Not just satisfied to do the best she could? That stubborn little voice in her heart, the one that urged her to look for rainbows and fairy rings, cried out.

Trey came immediately to mind. With his beautiful hands and teasing manner, he made her doubt herself. Those quick eyes and those clever lips were trouble. There was nothing dependable, nothing she could trust about this man. She didn't really know why he had changed his mind about helping her. She was afraid to ask why he had kissed her.

Ashley knew she should just put him from her mind. Yes, he had flirted with her. Just a little. And maybe she had flirted back. Just a little. Yes, he had kissed her. And she had kissed him. It had been devastating. Rainbows and fairy rings. When he held her close, she couldn't think. She forgot to breathe. It was too much. And he was the wrong man. She didn't want a romantic entanglement with him. Not that she had entertained even the remotest notion that they would . . . that anything would happen. The very idea brought a flush to her cheeks and a quick change of thought.

She did want to have a family of her own someday. That time would be gone before she had considered it, if she wasn't careful. She pictured a little boy with dark hair and laughing gray eyes. A younger version of Trey.

''No!'' she protested out loud.

The woman on the passenger's side of the car next to her stared up at her, then the light changed and the traffic moved on.

Hot exhaust mingled with the already heated, moist air that had moved up the coast to plague them. Ashley reached the open highway thankfully, putting the truck on cruise control and following the signs to Lexington.

She spent the time trying to reshape her vision of the future. She felt certain Rusty was going to ask her to make a definite commitment that weekend and she wanted to be prepared for her answer. The only answer, she reminded herself harshly, that she could rationally give him. Yes.

When she looked up again, the drive had slipped by before she was ready. As she saw the turnoff for Lexington airport, where the rally was held every year, she breathed a sigh of relief. Rusty wouldn't be up there until the next day. She had a long night to repeat the word ''yes'' enough times to convince herself.

Ashley had been going to the balloon rally every year since she could walk. She remembered every balloon they had ever raced, every color, all the designs.

She could remember her grandfather, very tall to her at the time, lifting her grandmother and her into the gondola. The fire had shot up into the balloon and they had lifted off the ground.

Her father had never had the same feeling for the balloons, although he continued the tradition. Bannister raced every year but her father hired teams, like Bobby Ferris's, to fly the balloons. Bobby had been racing the Bannister balloon for the past fifteen years. He was flamboyant, and at times utterly outrageous, but he was the best balloon pilot in the country.

The airport was littered with trucks and multicolored balloons in various stages of inflation. The green, flat, field, actually an old airport turned flea market, was stretched out like a quilt. Already the carnival people had finished their midway and were testing a few of the rides. There would be food vendors there for the two-day event and a local radio station was broadcasting live.

Ashley kept her eyes open as she followed the traffic through the gates at the entrance to the airport. She was looking for Bobby's distinctive red trucks but it appeared as though she had made it there before him.

"Howdy!"

"Hi!" she greeted the ticket taker at the gate. "Have you seen Bobby Ferris's team?"

"Haven't seen 'em yet," he told her. "That you, Miz Bannister?"

"It's me, Donnie."

"Wasn't sure." He laughed and his grizzled brown face cracked into a thousand lines. "You get prettier every year."

She grinned back at him. "And you tell 'em a little better every year!"

"You're right over there." He pointed, with a laugh. "Between the Shakey's balloon and Mighty Fine."

"Thanks," she replied.

She pulled the truck over to the area where the flag was staked into the sandy clay field, the Bannister name lettered in purple. There were markers where the other two balloon teams would be but they hadn't arrived yet. It seemed, she mused, turning off the engine, she would have had time to take that shower after all. She pushed back the seat and waited.

Ashley yawned as she watched the children already playing near the midway. Clowns in colored suits with orange and green hair laughed with them. The carnival tried out its lights, blinking them along the rides and signs. The sun was fading, blending the pale sky into the white clouds that hung along the horizon. A few balloons were being inflated to get ready for the next day. Their bright colors slowly grew, fluttering gently in the evening breeze.

She yawned again and glanced at her watch. Bobby should have been there. She would give him a while longer then walk up to the concession stand and use their phone.

She leaned her head back on the seat. Dawn was too early for anybody to be up, she decided, and still be awake that night. It had been a long, hard week. She was drained and beyond worrying about what was going to come next. What else could happen?

She was just going to close her eyes for a few minutes then go to the concession stand. A little rest and she would be able to get into the spirit of the weekend.

When Trey arrived two hours later, Bobby Ferris's team was already unloading the back of the truck. It was dark but the carnival lights illuminated Ashley's sleeping face in the open window.

She looked . . . peaceful. He knew she was at war with herself over having him work for her. It wasn't easy for her to let someone else make decisions. Her hair was like white silk in the light and his fingers burned to let the strands slide through them. He didn't know why he was there or why he had let her turn his well-ordered life into chaos.

He knew he was attracted her. More than he had been attracted to any other woman for a long time. It scared him. How much of that emotion was passion and how much could be twisted up with revenge?

He had never thought of himself as a vengeful man. After his failed attempt to compete with Parish Bannister, he had tried to put all of that life from his mind. It wasn't until she had come to him, straight shoulders and trusting blue eyes, that he had considered hurting Parish through his daughter.

But Parish was dead. Ashley wasn't her father. It was difficult to remember anything else when he looked at her face. Yet didn't they say it was a thin line between love and hate?

She stirred and sighed, then blinked her eyes. ''Trey?'' She made out his face in the colored lights.

''Hello, sleeping beauty!'' His voice was husky with emotion as he looked at her.

''How long have I been asleep?'' she wondered, feeling stiff. Her brain was muddled. She moved a little in the truck seat and found that both of her feet were numb.

''Since I've been here. Over an hour. Bobby said you were asleep when he got here and he hated to wake you.''

''Bobby's here?'' She frowned, trying to work the pins and needles out of her toes.

She wasn't really awake yet.

''He's all set up for tomorrow,'' Trey told her. ''They've gone somewhere to eat.''

Ashley couldn't believe she had slept through the crew taking the balloon off the back of the truck and setting up the rig. She had always been a light sleeper. Stress had apparently taken its toll. She started to climb out of the truck and winced when her foot hit the ground.

"Something wrong?" he wondered, hearing her sharply drawn breath.

She laughed self-consciously. "My feet are asleep."

"Sit back a minute," he recommended.

When she had resumed her place on the truck seat, Trey reached for her right foot and took off her shoe.

"It'll be fine in a minute," she assured him as he started to massage her foot.

"Massage is the best thing for bad circulation," he informed her. "My brother-in-law is a chiropractor."

His hands were strong and warm on the delicate contours of her ankle and the arch in her foot. A hot, sweet languor began to take over her, making her legs felt like wet spaghetti.

"It may be." She sighed. "But I don't know if it's going to be better for walking."

He smiled and reached across and started to work on her left foot. His dark head was so close as he leaned over her leg. It would be simple to reach out and touch him.

"Better?" he asked, looking up into her face.

"Much," she whispered, not able to look away.

"Ashley?"

Her confused gaze didn't stray. She wanted him to kiss her again. Not caring about the consequences.

He didn't wait for further invitation. His mouth touched hers lightly, as cool as a spring breeze.

Ashley's eyes opened and she looked at him in the strange light from the carnival. He was staring at her so intently that she felt like it should have hurt.

"You look like an angel," he murmured, threading his fingers through her hair as he'd wanted to do so many times.

She closed her eyes again when his hands pulled her closer. She slid against him as she slipped from the truck seat and he held her there.

"Trey," she said breathlessly, wrapping her arms around his neck, "I'm starving."

"Ashley," he responded, "I'm pretty hungry myself."

He kissed her again. The sparkling lights of the midway were no match for the lights that went off in her head when she gave in to his kiss.

"Hey, Ashley!" Bobby Ferris laughed from behind them. "I thought you'd never wake up!"

"Bobby!" she squealed uncomfortably, trying to move away from Trey. He stepped back and let her slide past him.

"Ashley, honey, you sure do look good! Where's that beau of yours?" Bobby demanded, hugging her.

"Rusty's back in Martinsville," she answered a little breathlessly, embarrassed at getting caught in Trey's arms.

"Well, he should be up here watching out for you!

One of these days, somebody's gonna come along and sweep you off your feet!''

"Only you." She laughed. "You're the only one crazy enough to try."

"Looks like someone else was trying pretty hard!" Bobby declared. "Do I know you, old son?"

"Trey Harris." He held out his hand to the other man.

Bobby nodded as he shook his hand and sized him up. "Nice to meet you." He pulled a man forward from behind him. "This is our new volunteer, Ashley."

"Jeff Satterfield." The man stretched out his hand to her. "I don't know what I'm doing here."

"You're here to bring us luck!" Bobby insisted. "Jeff runs a cruise ship in Wilmington. He and I used to race planes in the Air Force together before he settled down on the water."

"Safer than sailing through the skies in a basket," Jeff retorted.

Bobby laughed and slapped Jeff on the back.

"He's crazy, you know," Jeff assured Trey and Ashley. "This is my wife, Dana. And my sister, Penny."

"He's crazy, too," Dana added when she took Ashley's hand. "That's why we're all here."

"What about you?" Bobby turned to Trey again. "Like to try your hand in the gondola?"

"No, thanks." Trey shook his head. "I'm better with my feet on the ground."

"Nobody's better that way, old son," Bobby insisted.

"What about me, old son?" Ashley mimicked, pulling on his sleeve.

Bobby looked down from his lofty height, the hat perched on the top of his head making him look like an ostrich. His graying hair belied the youthfulness of his thin face.

"Ashley, honey, you can't be serious! Your father never went up."

"That was his mistake," she retorted. "If you think just because I run the company now that I'm not going up, think again. I suppose I could find someone else to race for us."

"Ooooh, you are cold, Ashley Bannister! A mean, cold woman!"

"Never mind all that stuff." She laughed. "Plan on me being there in the morning."

"I don't envy you having to work with her, Trey," Bobby told him solemnly.

"I don't envy you having to go up in a balloon with her," Trey replied in kind. "At least there's no place for me to fall."

Bobby liked that, laughing outrageously. "You'll do." A young woman in a matching silver team jacket joined him, her arm around his waist. "I'll be seeing all of you in the morning."

"What does he do when he's not racing balloons?" Trey wondered, amazed.

"Races cars," Jeff replied. "He says balloons are for the soul. He races cars for the money."

"Trey shook his head in amazement."

"I haven't eaten since this morning." Ashley turned to Jeff and Dana. "Would you like to join us for a snack?"

Jeff glanced at Dana and Penny. "We'd like that."

They ate at the only stand set up in the midway. It was nachos and burritos with some cinnamon apple crispies.

"When are you due?" Ashley asked Dana, whose pregnancy was clearly visible.

Dana finished eating a third apple crispie. "Two months. I already feel like a whale."

Jeff wrapped an arm around her shoulders. "You're the best-looking whale I've ever seen."

She smiled up at him. "Thanks."

"Ugh!" Penny grimaced. "Can I walk around the carnival?"

Jeff nodded then watched the girl walk away. "Sometimes . . ."

"Teenagers," Ashley sympathized.

"I guess we should follow," Jeff began.

Dana tossed away the paper container that had held her cinnamon crispies. "Guess again. Give her some room to breathe! I think we should go walk around and we'll meet her later."

Jeff grimaced. "We've only been married a year."

"And already he's my willing slave." Dana grinned and waved to Ashley. "It was nice to meet you."

"Thanks." Ashley laughed. "You, too. See you tomorrow."

"Nice couple," Trey remarked, tossing aside the last of his burrito. "Great cheekbones."

"Always the artist?" she asked, starting to walk down the midway. It was after midnight but she was too exhilarated by the night to sleep.

Trey fell into step beside her. "Is there a thing going on between you and Rusty Lee that I should know about?"

She stopped and faced him. "That doesn't answer my question."

"No," he agreed. "But it's more interesting."

"I don't think my relationship with Rusty has anything to do with our working relationship."

Trey started walking again and Ashley ran to catch up with him.

"Since I started sculpting, I look at everything differently. I guess everyone and everything is a possible model." He glanced at her. "Your turn."

She shook her head slowly, not taking her eyes from his face. "Not exactly. Rusty and I have been close, I guess. Everyone just expects something to happen between us."

"What do you expect?" he asked seriously, taking her hand in his.

"I—I don't know," she replied breathlessly. "Rainbows and fairy rings?"

"There's nothing wrong with that," he told her quietly, tucking a strand of hair behind her ear, trailing his finger down her jawline. "You're a special person. You have the right to expect special things."

His voice and his touch were doing special things to her pulse and her mental processes. She had to find a way to be more professional with him.

"What are you doing up here?" she asked finally, when she had control of her heart and her voice.

"You looked like you needed some company," he answered as though it were the most natural thing in the world.

Ashley turned away and didn't reply. She was afraid of being incoherent again as she tried to digest his words. He'd just wanted to be with her.

"The balloon looks good," he replied, making conversation with the first thing that came to mind. "It's hard to believe how big it is until you're up close to it."

Trey bought them coffee in paper cups and elephant ears rolled in powdered sugar as they sat at a picnic table and watched a bluegrass fiddler tuning his instrument.

"Are you all right?" he asked, looking at her profile against the sprinkling of lights around the field.

"I'm fine," she replied quickly. "Maybe a little out of it. I'm still not sure how I slept through six men taking a balloon out of the back of the truck."

"My grandpa would've said it was the sleep of the innocent," he supplied. "When I got here, Bobby was standing outside the truck window looking at you like he wasn't sure what to do."

"And I was snoring." She snickered.

"Maybe just a little," he retorted, swallowing the rest of his coffee.

The fiddler, his fiddle tuned to his satisfaction, proceeded into a sweet violin concerto that would have brought tears to a statue's eyes. It happened at a moment when everything and everyone else had fallen silent. The final notes sang out and lingered in the darkness and the quiet, then the spell was broken. A new group of screaming children took a turn on the Tilt-A-Whirl and a hot drumbeat shook the sound system on the stage.

The little bearded fiddler looked up and shrugged, laughing, before launching into a foot-stomping bluegrass tune.

Ashley found herself staring at Trey, looking at the light reflected in his eyes. What was it she saw there?

"Did I miss something?" he asked, looking back at her, a smile flirting with his lips.

"People are full of surprises." Ashley managed to look away, pulling her gaze from his with an effort. "Thanks for coming up."

"Ashley—"

"I think we should call it a night," she decided abruptly. She started to get up from the picnic table but her foot slid on a patch of wet grass.

Without thinking, Trey caught her, pulling her back against him. He felt her heart racing in her chest. Her breath came in shallow gulps.

Ashley put out her hands for leverage and found

them on his jean-covered thighs. Undaunted, she turned back to him to apologize but before she could form the words, one of his hands were in her hair, the other touching her face.

"All right," he murmured, his face moving closer to hers. "I'm surprised. You're right. I never thought this could happen to me." He kissed her lightly, barely touching, giving her the opportunity to pull away.

Ashley, wondering if he had known what she was thinking on the drive up from Martinsville, returned his caress. The storm of emotion that her tentative kiss unleashed made her shiver. His lips moved over hers possessively, seeking the warmth of her mouth. His long, clever fingers feathered through her hair, bringing her closer to him.·

Ashley shifted slightly and sighed. She couldn't move. Her feet were dangling at an impossible angle from the bench. His head was on his chest, his arms wrapped around her. She wanted it to go on forever but a voice in her head was persistent.

What was she doing? What had happened to all of her good intentions?

The answer was simple. When she was around Trey, she had no good intentions. She simply fell apart, refused to think, and let him kiss her or bully her into doing what he wanted her to do with the company. It was impossible.

"This has to stop," she said finally, lifting her head to look into his face.

"Any particular reason?" he wondered, feeling distinctly colder than he had been a few minutes earlier.

"We work together. We don't have a relationship. You aren't even sure you don't hate me through my father." She listed the reasons that came to mind.

Gray eyes assessed her flushed face. "You're scared. You don't trust me. It's easier to fall back on a sure thing."

Ashley squirmed a little then looked at him again. "Will you help me up?"

"Sure," he agreed, helping her to her feet. "Will you be honest with me?"

She nodded, shoving her hands into her pockets.

"If we had just met, would things be different?"

"I don't know,' she answered thoughtfully. "I really don't know."

"Where are you staying?" he wondered, trying to bring the conversation around to the mundane though he felt like someone had kicked him. He had asked for honesty.

She glanced at him. "I'm staying in the back of the pickup. It's easier than leaving and coming back."

"I can see that," he imagined. "Sleep in the back of a truck, under the stars, waiting for the dawn."

"There's a motel just up the highway from here," she told him with a sad smile. "There's probably plenty of room."

"But I might miss the balloon liftoff," he speculated.

"You might." She shrugged. "I'm afraid I only brought enough supplies for one."

They had reached the side of the pickup. It was dark and strangely quiet after the noise that had been around them. The balloon teams had started small campfires where they sat, some singing or talking, others already asleep.

Trey looked out into the darkness and smiled slowly, not willing to give up yet. "Luckily, France told me how the balloon team sleeps and I came prepared."

"You mean you want to sleep out here?" She couldn't believe her ears.

"Yup. I brought a small tent and a blanket. I'll set up right by the truck," he answered, his voice a little more quiet with the silence of the night around them. "It'll be an adventure."

Chapter Six

"All right," she assented briskly, climbing up into the back of the truck. "Suit yourself."

"Thanks." He started over to his car to get his gear. "Where does Bobby's racing team sleep?"

"Bobby doesn't," Ashley answered as she rolled out her sleeping bag in the bed of the truck. "Everybody else fends for themselves."

Trey starting setting up his one-man tent and his few supplies. From somewhere in the darkness, the bluegrass fiddle player's sound still cried against the chirp of crickets and the rush of the breeze in the leaves. A group of balloon racers quietly sang "Amazing Grace" around their dimming campfire and the smell of roasting food was everywhere.

Ashley was silent as she listened to Trey carefully setting up his tent next to the track. Her heart was beating fast. Why had he stayed there with her? The possible answers made her nervous and uneasy. She held herself in a tight knot inside her sleeping bag, waiting.

Trey lay down in his tent, with his head at the opening so he could see the night sky. The stars were bright overhead, billions of tiny points of light dancing in the black sky.

"You never appreciate the night until you're out of the city," he said quietly. "The sky is really black. Not orange or gray."

"You're different than I thought you'd be," she confided in the darkness. "My father talked about you, you know. If he could have had a son—"

"I'll take that as a compliment," he answered tautly. Any mention of Parish made him angry. "Although if he'd treated his son the same way—"

"He was wrong," she said simply. "He knew it when you were gone."

"Especially after Johnny left?"

"Before Johnny left," she assured him. "He never had the rapport with Johnny that he'd had with you."

Trey couldn't find a reply to that statement. She'd poured salt in an old wound as casually as she'd told him that she wasn't sure how she felt about him.

She turned on her side as if to face him, though he was a few feet away and in the blackness. "Why did you leave, Trey? I know why you left the company, but why did you leave town?"

He sighed, the memories bitter in his mind. "I

worked myself into a hole for your father. I had no life outside the factory. I threw myself into creating a rival company that could hurt your father for what he did to me. I spent night and day worrying about every detail, until one night on my way home, I fell asleep at the wheel and drove into a tree.''

He heard her catch her breath, and he smiled. There was that soft heart again. No, she wasn't like her father. ''I wasn't seriously hurt but it made me take a look at my life. I realized that what I was doing was stupid and I packed up and left Martinsville. It was the only way I could clear my mind of what had happened.''

Ashley was shaken. ''And you started sculpting?''

He laughed, softly, a sound that made her shiver. ''That was a fluke. My hand was broken in the crash and a therapist suggested working with soft clay as a way to strengthen it. I worked at a restaurant in New York that put artwork on display and sold it on commission. It was the beginning of a new life for me.''

''Then you came back here and I tracked you down and wanted you to relive your nightmare.''

He didn't reply but Ashley felt the need to go on anyway. ''You're still very good at management,'' she admitted ruefully, feeling she owed him some thanks for what he'd agreed to do for the company.

''But you don't like it,'' he whispered into the night between them.

It wasn't strictly true, she considered, although she didn't say it. When David had asked for help in finding sewing machines, Trey had found what he needed, and most important, found a way to get them. "I don't need to like it."

"That's probably true," he allowed. "I do what needs to be done. That's not always popular."

"I do appreciate what you've done."

"That was a hard thing to admit," he appreciated in return.

"I read the papers," she said quietly. "I know Bannister stock went up with the announcement of the company hiring you as a consultant."

And that, too, was a bitter pill to swallow. All of her life, Ashley had done the best she could for the company. With just his name, Trey Harris had made Bannister more attractive and probably convinced some people to think about renewing old contracts.

"We can work together on this, Ashley," he continued in the darkness, wishing he could see her. Not daring to cross the span between them and touch her.

"How?" she demanded. "I thought you'd made it very clear that you have to work alone."

"I admit it. I've never been in the position to share responsibility with anyone. And neither have you."

He was right, of course. When her father was alive, his word was law. Since her father's death, she had taken over every aspect of the company. It wasn't that she was afraid to ask for advice or that she didn't respect David's opinion. It was more that she knew that the decision and the result was ultimately on her head.

"All right." She swept her hand through the air. "I don't know if we can survive a meeting of our minds, but I'm willing to try."

"I think it can work. And it'll keep me from having to relearn all those complicated sewing machine terms."

"Was this just a sneaky way to get me to do your work?" She laughed at the sky above her, feeling suddenly lighthearted.

"No," he confessed, a hand under his head. "It was a sneaky way to tell you that I finished putting in a new computer system at the plant today."

"You've corrupted Frances." She shook her head slowly over the sad turn of events.

"Some women find me irresistible," he teased.

"Mmm," she murmured, listening to the hushed sound of the wind and the call of the birds that filled the night around them.

"Ashley?" he whispered after a moment.

When there was no reply, he strained to hear any sound from the dark figure in the truck bed. There was no mistaking the soft sound of her breathing.

"And some women just go to sleep," he muttered quietly. "Good night, Ashley. Dream of me."

When Trey awakened the next morning, the rally was already well under way and Ashley was gone.

"She left with the balloon at first light," Frances told him, sitting on the tailgate, calmly eating cookies. She pointed toward the sky. "There they are."

In the far, hazy distance, Trey could barely make out the bright purple of the Bannister balloon. The pale blue sky was filled with balloons. All shapes, from the traditional pear shape to cartoon characters, and every color, had filled the sky. Some were just overhead, their gondolas filled with people. Most, like the Bannister balloon, were well away.

"Are they winning?" he wondered, not certain how to judge the winner in that race.

"It's difficult to say," Frances, a veteran balloon rally watcher, admitted. "Here." She handed him a pair of binoculars. "You can still see Ashley and Bobby."

Trey looked through the high-powered eyeglasses and found he could make out Ashley in her purple team shirt, standing beside Bobby Ferris in the gondola. "How far do they have to go?" He kept the binoculars to his eyes until he couldn't make out Ashley's face. Wispy clouds obscured the balloon as it dipped down into a valley.

"Don't worry," Frances apprised him kindly. "You have plenty of time to eat and talk sweet to the stockholders before she gets back."

Trey looked out at the distant, disappearing specks of color and grabbed his backpack.

"Give me five minutes to clean up and I'm ready to go."

Frances watched him stretch his back painfully.

"I'll give you an extra five to be able to get that

kink out of your back.'' She laughed. ''That tent of yours wasn't exactly the Ritz, I bet.''

The day was warm and sunny. Blue skies and smiles were all around the group that continued to grow as the morning progressed. Trey's confident face and firm handshake were everywhere as he smiled at the ladies and talked sports with the men. Several stockholders expressed their concerns and were impressed by the working team that David Baxter and Trey Harris presented.

''It's not that we don't trust Ashley,'' one woman confided as she looked at her husband. ''It's just that the stock has declined.''

''I think we can make it worth your while to keep that stock,'' Trey told her. ''Between Ashley and me, there isn't anything we don't know about this business.''

Frances passed out the flyers that Trey had wanted her to print up. They underscored everything that had been happening within the company, including hiring him as management consultant and the new contract with Tagami Corporation.

Trey glanced at his watch in the hot sun, looking around himself in the middle of the crowd. It was nearly noon and there was still no sign of Ashley. He was starting to get annoyed.

Ashley came in on the first available transport back from the landing site. She'd left Bobby and his crew to get the balloon together and had come back with the other chase vehicle.

Bobby hadn't exactly applauded her decision to cut out on them without doing any of the work, but Ashley had been adamant. Conscious of the ever-growing time lapse since she'd left with the balloon that morning, she spent the ride back chastising herself for having left Trey alone. If things got messed up at that sensitive juncture, she would have only herself to blame.

Jumping from the mud-splashed Jeep as soon as it stopped, the first thing she saw was David and Trey laughing with Tom Conaway, an important stockholder who'd been a good friend of her father. There were yellow and purple flyers everywhere. She scanned one quickly and found that Trey had covered it all. If she had known that he could handle it without her, she would have waited for Bobby!

Watching him, even knowing that he was schmoozing, it was hard to find anything artificial about Trey. He seemed to genuinely enjoy what he did, laughing with Tom and David, listening to the workers in the plant. She'd noticed it even though she hadn't really liked it. She hadn't expected to like him. In fact, she had started out determined *not* to like him. He was everything she'd always despised in the business world—hard, ruthless. He should have been shallow, phony, full of himself, but though he made her mad, she couldn't fault him when it came to job dedication. Trey zeroed in on his mark and went for it like a guided missile!

"He's really something," Rusty observed, with a

glass of lemonade for her in his free hand and a quick kiss on her cheek.

"He is," she agreed, taking the glass, wondering how Trey managed to look so fresh after spending the night on the ground. She felt dusty and tired, not really up to the festivities that still remained that day.

She looked at Rusty in his fresh green sports shirt and khaki shorts then at Trey in his clean white shirt and blue jeans. She needed a shower and a change of clothes.

"And you honestly believe that he can save the company?" Rusty continued, still watching Trey as he talked with a group from the warehouse section of the plant.

"I think he can buy me some time, maybe even scare off Marshall and Seymour." She pushed a weary hand through her windblown hair. "I don't know. But I can't just give up without trying everything. I think you know me that well."

"I know." He put his arm around her shoulders and hugged her close. "You look exhausted, honey. Let me get you something to eat and find a place you can rest."

"Ashley?" Trey finally made his way across the field to her. He frowned when he saw Rusty's head bent down close to hers, his arms around her. Something uncomfortably like jealousy bit him deeply.

She turned back to face him. "Trey, I—"

"She's exhausted, Harris. She needs to rest," Rusty

proclaimed belligerently. He pulled Ashley closer to him.

"She needs to get cleaned up and get over here with David and me," Trey told him angrily, though his eyes were concentrated on Ashley's face. "I've been waltzing around questions all morning for her."

"You'll just have to dance alone a little longer." Rusty's arm tightened on her shoulder. "She's not up to it right now."

"Not up to it?" Trey demanded. "Then she had no business going up in the first place."

"Will you both please be quiet for a minute?" Ashley intervened.

Both men glared at her. The sun beat down on Rusty's light brown head, a good three inches taller than Trey's. Trey's hair was darker, even in the bright sun, and while his shoulders were broad, they were much more slender than Rusty's. If it came to a fight between the two men, she wasn't sure which man would win. She didn't want to find out.

Ashley looked at both of them, instantly separating the two men by what she knew of each one. There was a certain look in Trey's eyes that reminded her of the fact that he had been brought up fighting for what he wanted. Rusty, on the other hand, had the complacent look of a man who'd always had it all.

"I'm going to change," she told Trey as she disengaged herself from Rusty's arm. "And I can speak for myself, Rusty."

"Ashley, don't let him bully you," Rusty urged her,

ready to knock the other man down. "You're the boss. He works for you."

Ashley noticed that they were attracting attention to the group. Several interested shareholders, as well as her mother and Frances, were watching them. "Never mind, Rusty," she whispered, pulling him aside as she started to walk away. "I'll be there in a few minutes," she promised Trey, leaving him standing in the interested throng.

Ashley didn't need to see his bright eyes to feel them boring into her back as she walked away with Rusty. That he was angry, she had little doubt. No one could look into those eyes and hear the tone of his voice without being singed.

"You're going to have to keep him in line," Rusty said in a voice that didn't bother to hide that fact that he thought he'd been triumphant in the exchange.

"I'll thank you to stay out of what Trey and I have to say to each other," she deflated him. "This is business, Rusty."

"And as your fiancé—"

"Which you aren't yet," she reminded him.

"C'mon, Ashley." He smiled and started to pull her to him. "We've known each other too long for these games."

"And even if you were my husband," she finished, aware that his maneuvering was for Trey's benefit, "some things have nothing to do with you. I wouldn't interfere in what you do."

Rusty couldn't believe his ears. "Ashley," he began, his blue eyes wide in his red face, "if you won't give me any consideration as the man you might marry, maybe I can get your attention as a major stockholder!"

"All right," she answered calmly, ignoring Trey's interested gaze as he stood in the distance. "What do you want me to do?"

"Fire that man! There's nothing he can do for Bannister. Let's just sell out to Marshall and Seymour and get married."

"Rusty, I hired Trey because I thought he could help, and he's already done some good. As a stockholder, trust me for a little longer. We're going to win this thing and come out better."

"Ashley—"

"And as the man I *might* marry, you're going to have to understand that I have a job to do. That has to be something you like about me or we can't have a future together."

Rusty's eyes were warm as he quickly kissed her lips. "I do understand. And I love you for it. And I want the wedding to be as soon as possible."

"We'll see when this is straightened out with the company," she promised, feeling a knot form in the pit of her stomach.

It was for the best, she told herself as he hugged her. Once the plans were being made, there wouldn't be any more doubts. And no more temptation.

Rusty kissed her quickly again then left her at the

door to Bobby's RV where she'd changed her clothes that morning.

Ashley changed quickly, washed her face, and brushed her hair. She whisked an imaginary speck from her white shirt and matching white cotton pants. The outfit showed off her light tan and made her hair seem very bright. She looked at her blue eyes in the mirror as she smoothed on some lip gloss. For just a minute, she thought about the night before and the feel of Trey's lips on hers. She thought about his deep voice telling her things she didn't think he'd shared with many other people.

When she'd left that morning, sneaking out of the back of the truck carefully so she wouldn't wake him, she'd watched him for a minute. His hair was wind-blown, his eyelashes dark against his cheeks, his nose very straight. She'd imagined pressing her lips to his for just an instant, wondered about touching the scar by his mouth and asking where he'd got it.

Then she'd felt the chill of the morning air feather down her spine, and some measure of common sense had pushed itself into her brain.

Together, they might be able to save the company. That had to be the only thing between them. Then she would marry Rusty Lee. Sturdy, reliable Rusty, and she would live a good life. No surprises. No disappointments. And no excitement, a treacherous part of her mind told her. No passion. No rainbows or fairy rings.

"Shut up," she said aloud to her reflection in the mirror, then left Bobby's RV.

It wasn't hard to find him. Trey's dark head was a little taller than the people around him at that point. He was involved in deep conversation with Frank Wilson and another man she didn't recognize. If lightning could have shot from those intent eyes, she realized, the other two men would have been seriously injured. He had an aggressive chin and a stance that made him seem as though he were about to vibrate. Maybe that was part of the passion that everyone saw in his sculptures. His energy brought a vibrancy to everything around him.

"Gentlemen." She approached, noticing at once that the men were uncomfortable with their conversation around her. What had they been talking about, for heaven's sake, that they wouldn't want her to hear? The men changed topics the minute she reached them, Frank Wilson going totally silent until he left a minute later.

When the other gray-haired man, who introduced himself as Walter Rauchelle, had excused himself, Trey glanced at her, then walked away.

"Wait a minute." She stopped him, putting a hand on his arm. "What was that all about?"

"Business, remember?" he taunted her softly.

"I'm sorry I left you here alone with it."

"No problem, boss," he replied quickly. "That's what I'm here for, right?"

He turned again and started to walk away until Ashley grabbed his arm and brought him around to face her. "I didn't say that I expected you to do everything," she explained, trying to keep her sudden flash of anger under control. "Rusty didn't understand."

"Did you have enough time to explain it to him?" he asked nastily.

"That's none of your business," she flared. "Look, I'm sorry about being gone for so long. We got blown off course or I would've been back sooner. As for Rusty, he was just trying to stand up for me."

"Hey, I don't need an explanation." He held up a hand, an unpleasant smile on his face. "I just work here. Excuse me, I see some other stockholders I haven't met."

Ashley stared after him as he melted into the crowd that was increasing as the balloon teams rejoined the group.

"Men!" Frances sighed, giving out the last flyer she'd brought with her to an elderly woman walking by them.

"I'm going to eat lunch," Ashley told her, consigning Trey to the nether regions. "Want to come?"

They found a nice table near an old magnolia tree. Its dark green, shiny leaves and white flowers hovered near their heads as they sat down.

"I think things have gone very well today," Frances started, setting up her plate and plastic eating utensils.

"I really didn't plan on being back so late," Ashley murmured defensively, batting away a fly from her plate. "Bobby couldn't hold the balloon in the cross breeze and we had to go farther than we'd planned."

"David and Trey handled everything fine." Frances told her. "Don't worry. Everyone here remembers that Bannister Balloons are what we're famous for and they understand."

Ashley pushed a pickle around on her plate with her fork. "I know. I just hope this was the right thing to do."

"Trey, you mean?" Frances guessed, with a nod of her carefully coiffed head. "Well, it seems to be working."

Ashley nodded. "It certainly does."

Frances looked up, picking up on Ashley's line of vision.

Trey was carrying plates of food for himself and Margaret Bannister, her wide straw hat brim bouncing as she walked toward them. Her flowing flowered skirt and bright pink blouse made a quaint summer portrait against the green grass and blue sky.

"What a glorious day!" Margaret beamed, breathing deeply. She cleaned off a bit of space on the picnic bench with a white handkerchief.

Trey put down their plates on the table then sat beside her on the bench opposite Ashley and Frances.

Margaret looked at Ashley and Trey's carefully averted heads. "I thought we should sit together. I hope that's all right?"

"That's fine." Frances nodded, digging into her food. "This slaw is really great."

"And the corn is exceptional this year," Margaret commented, daintily tasting her from her plate.

Ashley murmured something unintelligible. Trey made no reply at all. Margaret and Frances glanced at each other across the table. A friend of Margaret's joined them and the three women began a spirited conversation about their high school days.

Trey had finished eating by the beginning of the exchange and was getting to his feet. Ashley was on hers and after him before he got up the grassy hill.

"Trey, I'm sorry." She caught up with him. "Will you listen to me?"

He stopped walking abruptly and she came up face to face with him.

"Ashley," he started, then thought better, the morning eyes losing their killer glint. "I'm sorry, too, for those stupid cracks. What you do with Rusty is none of my business. I was just mad about you being gone so long."

"Are you sure?" she asked, wanting to take a step back but finding herself on the steep incline of the hill.

"About what?" He smiled, his eyes faithfully following every line of her face.

"You and Rusty seem—"

He shrugged and started walking. "We seem like two men who don't trust each other."

Ashley walked beside him up the hill to throw away her plate and cup. "You just don't know each other."

"I don't expect to be friends with Rusty."

She looked across at him, the sun bright on his face.

"I suppose not." She didn't need to ask why. The enmity between the two men was obvious and it had little to do with the company. "Not that it matters," she concluded brightly. "He's a little overprotective around you right now but I'm sure he'll get over it."

"Are you?" he wondered. He took a step closer to her, his gaze caressing her lips and her face as though he had touched her. "Why?

Chapter Seven

Ashley faltered as everything else seemed to fall away. She was drawn to him, fascinated by the light playing over his face.

"I think he's just a little . . . uncertain," she replied weakly, fighting that strange sense of warmth and confusion that had come over her.

"Till he gets that ring on your finger?" he quipped lightly, though there was no smile on his face.

"I don't think that's fair," she responded. "Rusty has always been a good friend to me."

"I overheard him telling your mother that you had finally agreed to marry him," he acknowledged. "Congratulations."

Ashley looked away. "Thanks."

They watched a tethered balloon glide slowly into

the sky with its load of small children. The bright red pear shape was brilliant against the blue sky.

"When's the happy day?" he wondered, looking back at her.

"I don't know," she returned, wishing he would change the subject. "Sometime later in the year, or next year, I suppose."

"Once you're sure about the company?"

"Something like that." She smiled at him. "You did a great job this morning."

"That's what you hired me for," he repeated.

"I know you've done more than that," she told him, "and I know that it's working."

"Thanks," he answered warmly. "We have a long way to go."

Ashley agreed. "I know."

"No ring yet?" He took her hand in his. "Rusty's taking some chances."

"No one's coming along to sweep me off my feet," she promised him soundly.

His eyes glinted wickedly. "Really?" He used his grip on her hand to tug her toward him. "Competition is always healthy, Ashley."

"In business," she reminded him when his face was close to hers. She held her breath and let her eyes close as he lowered his head to hers.

"I suppose you're right," he conceded, his breath touching her lips. He drew back and looked at her. "If you really love Rusty, I wouldn't do anything that would come between you."

Ashley opened her eyes. He was very close. There was no way, facing him in the bright sunlight, that she could pretend to be unaffected. Her heart was pounding and her throat was dry. "I—I—"

"Do you love him, Ashley?" he asked softly, still holding her hand.

"I don't know," she replied feebly. "We've known each other for so long."

"You've said that before," he reminded her. "Does that substitute for love?"

She shook her head and looked away from his intense gaze. "I don't know."

"What about rainbows and fairy rings?"

"I did that once. I know Rusty. He's safe."

"Safe?" he questioned, dropping her hand to grasp her shoulders. "I wouldn't have thought you would settle for safe, Ashley!"

She looked up at him again. His eyes were stormy and his mouth was a grim line. "Safe is better than sorry," she quipped at him.

"Coward," he replied earnestly. "How can you be so brave for Bannister and not for yourself?"

"Ashley?" A voice hailed her. "Am I interrupting?"

Max Spenser and his wife were standing under the tree beside them, watching them, with smiles playing across their features.

"Max," Ashley answered awkwardly. She smiled at the couple then turned to Trey. "Have you met Max Spenser and his wife yet?"

"I don't think so," he replied, wishing he could have met them a little later.

Max Spenser was actually a competitor of theirs from Tennessee. A self-made millionaire, he'd bought a large block of Bannister stock as a young man.

To hold over his head, Ashley's father had always told her.

"Trey Harris, this is Max Spenser." Ashley approached him. "And this is his wife, Elena."

"Ashley!" Elena Spenser's smooth, white face wrinkled sweetly when she smiled. "How good to see you!"

"So this is your golden boy." Max didn't dissemble, looking Trey over with a practiced eye. "I remember you. You were Parish's biggest mistake."

"I agree," Trey spoke up suddenly after shaking hands with the older man.

"Love you, Ashley," Max told her briefly. "But your father was a fool not to see it."

"That's why I hired him back," Ashley told the man. "He's still good at what he does."

Max snorted. "All I've seen so far this morning is a lot of sweet talk and pretty pictures. Where's the substance?"

"Mr. Spenser," Trey replied at the older man's insistence, "let's talk shop."

Elena and Ashley walked together with the two men behind immersed in "shop talk."

"What a wonderful day for the rally," Elena said, listening with half an ear to Trey's dazzling words.

"It did turn out nice," Ashley agreed with a ready smile. Elena had always been one of her favorite people.

"And what a gorgeous man!" The older woman lowered her voice and laughed, her pale blue eyes darting back to Trey.

"He's very . . . competent," Ashley replied carefully.

"I'm sure he is." Elena laughed again.

"We're trying to talk business here, if you don't mind," Max interrupted his wife.

"Not at all," Elena told him, raising her eyebrows at Ashley. "He's such an old bear!"

"He doesn't know much about balloons," Max told Ashley over her shoulder. "Guess you have to teach him, huh?"

"He doesn't really need to know much about sewing or balloons, Max," Ashley protested. "He knows about money and making the plant run more efficiently."

"You can't fix something if you don't understand what's broken!"

Ashley and Trey exchanged guarded looks.

Music from the midway area combined with the laughter of children going up and down in the tethered balloons. The line was still long for the roasting pit and the breeze blew the good food smell across the flat airport grounds and into the tree-shaded hillside.

"I'm getting hungry, Max," Elena told him, taking his arm. "Let's get some lunch."

"In a minute," Max told her, waving her hand away from his arm.

"I think with us working together on the project, our combined knowledge will be enough," Trey answered, knowing Max was waiting for an answer.

Ashley agreed quickly. "And there isn't anything I don't know about balloons. Or sewing."

"And you want to impress me with that?" Max turned away. "We might as well have that lunch now, Elena."

"What else do you want, Max?" Ashley asked impatiently.

Max Spenser turned back to face the two young people, his wily eyes appraising them both. *No doubt to see how far he can push us,* Ashley considered.

"Has the boy even been up?" he wondered.

She glanced at Trey. "No."

"What?" Max exploded. "And you expect him to help you make balloons?"

"He doesn't have to be in a car accident to make air bags for cars, does he?" Ashley demanded in turn.

"Or skydive to make parachutes?" Elena asked helpfully, nodding at her friend.

"I'll go up," Trey said firmly.

"You don't have to," Ashley told him, noticing that the two men were standing, staring eye-to-eye.

"I'm not afraid to go up," he answered flatly. "I just haven't had time."

"But you don't have to let him tell you what to do," Ashley assured him. "Max is always—"

"Ashley." He stopped her. "I'll go up."

Max nodded curtly then smiled, reaching for his wife's arm. "I believe we can go to lunch now," he told her briskly. "And, of course, we wouldn't think of selling our shares, Ashley! You know us better than that!"

"Nice meeting you, Max." Trey shook his hand.

"I expect to see my stock triple in the next year, son."

"No doubt." Trey smiled slightly.

"Going up will do you good." Max clapped him on the back. "Ashley, good to see you."

"Max, you can't just—"

"I'll send you pictures of the trip," Trey told him.

"I look forward to it."

Ashley stood her ground as Elena and Max made for the lunch line. "What now?"

He shrugged. "Now, I go up in a balloon."

"You don't have to do this," Ashley told him angrily. "You don't have to prove anything to Max! He's not going to sell out or anything."

"Hey, I'm the risk taker, remember?" he asked with a laugh. "And maybe Max is right. Maybe you do need to go up to understand. The way I see it now, the balloon division of Bannister should be shut down."

"What!?" she demanded, pulling him back by the shoulder. His shirt was warm to her hand. "What are you saying? Bannister *is* balloons. Everyone knows that."

"The company loses money making balloons and has every year for the past ten years," he returned heatedly. "What were you and your father thinking about? You're supposed to be in business to make money."

"There's more to business than just making money," she told him defiantly. "Bannister is balloons."

"Bannister is nothing without making a profit!"

They faced each other in the hot sunshine, squaring off on opposite ends of the quarrel.

"Fine," she relented, seeing that he wouldn't be moved. "I'll take you up myself."

He looked doubtful. "Maybe it would be better if Bobby—"

"Never mind," she rejected his idea. "I've been a pilot since I was sixteen. They shoot off fireworks tonight. We'll go up and be back before then. I'll set it up."

"It might not make any difference," he warned as she started to walk away. "The balloons still don't make any money."

"Just be there an hour from now," she answered. "Don't forget your camera."

Ashley found Bobby in the crowd around the ice cream–making competition. It wasn't hard to convince him that she meant to take the balloon up herself. It wasn't the first time, just the first time since her father had died.

"I'll have the crew set it up." He nodded. "I

thought you'd never go up again after your daddy died. Guess I was wrong.''

Ashley hadn't told him her motivation but he'd laughed when she told him her passenger was Trey Harris. ''Think he can handle it?'' Bobby wondered, lighting a cigar.

''We'll find out.'' She shrugged. ''See you later.''

She found a place in the shade that was away from the noise and the crowd. Back against a wooden rail, her arms around her knees, she watched the Easy Coax Briquets people bringing in their balloon. It was shaped like a bag of their charcoal.

She knew each group's designs, all their colors. Every balloon crew had their own design that no one else copied. Some were even patented. She'd been around ballooning all her life. It was as much a part of her as driving a car or eating cold ice cream on a hot summer's day.

The idea that Trey would seriously want to stop making balloons was outrageous. Yes, she had agreed there might be some things he would want to do that she wouldn't like. But she wouldn't let him kill the balloon-making part of their company. It was as though he'd suggested cutting off her arm!

How could she make him understand? Not that he could do anything without her approval. Nothing that drastic. He could try to make the other stockholders pressure her.

Maybe Rusty was right, she considered. Maybe she had let in the lion. If so, it was too late to undo that decision. Now she had to find a way to minimize the damage. It was her company, after all. She had to pull herself together, start thinking like a Bannister! Trey was more experienced in management but she knew her own business. And she hadn't fought like a demon the past year since her father had died to let him drive it into the ground.

A light breeze sighed through the tall grasses and the tree branches dipped slightly as though acknowledging the presence. Did everything have to change at once? She sighed with the summer breezes. Her life had gone along, if not ideally, then smoothly. Then in the space of a year, she'd lost her father and was teetering on losing her business.

Rusty, who'd always been content with their relationship the way it was, suddenly was kissing her in parking lots and demanding they set a date to be married.

And, of course, she couldn't forget Trey!

In the short time she'd known him, he had made her question more about her life than she had in the past ten years. He had chewed her out and spun her around. Not to mention kissing her nearly senseless. He'd made her think about things she thought she would never think about again and dream things that she wasn't sure she was better off not dreaming.

And where would it end? Trey would take his share of the profits when the company was out of danger. She would probably marry Rusty and probably, someday, sell the company she'd fought so hard to keep.

A little girl in blue jeans and a white tank top was begging her mother for a ride on the tethered balloon. The mother, a worried look on her young face, told the girl that it wasn't something that nice little girls did.

It wasn't hard for Ashley to imagine her mother telling her something similar when she was small and her grandfather overruling her with his gruff, cigar-smoking voice.

One thing at a time, he'd taught her when they were getting the balloon ready to fly. It never paid to get ahead of yourself. That way, it was easier to make mistakes. Keep your mind on the task at hand. And that was what she was going to do. Her first task was finding a way to win Trey over on the balloon issue. She could fight him but she needed her energy for more important things. She wanted him to be on her side.

Once they were over that hurdle, she could go on to the next. Whatever that would be, she smiled a little, running her hand through her hair. She wished she had clipped it to the back of her head. It was hot on her neck and would be a nuisance when they went up.

Ashley went to Bobby's RV to change back into her jeans and T-shirt. Ballooning wasn't meant for the pilot to be wearing white and expecting to stay clean. Handling a balloon took planning and careful attention to detail. It wouldn't do to have to worry about her hair or her clothes when the balloon was being caught by a wind current.

Finding a green hair clip in her purse, she secured her hair back from her face. After all, she needed to be on her best mettle if she was going to impress Trey. From what she'd seen of him, he was not a man easily impressed or swayed. Already a plan of sorts was forming in her brain. It included that rush of adrenaline that came with the balloon ascent and the feel of moving along the ground like a cloud. It was hard to imagine any human with an imagination who could resist that sensation!

If she had stopped to think about it, it might have bothered her that Trey's approval meant so much to her. As it was, she argued with herself that she didn't need to prove anything to him. He wasn't that important. He didn't have anything to do with the balloons anyway.

"We're waiting for you, Ashley!" Bobby urged her out of the RV door. "Just like a woman! In there primping for someone special!"

"Trey isn't exactly someone special," she scoffed. "Unless you consider that he thinks we should stop making balloons!"

"No!" Bobby was horrified.

"So I'm taking him up to, uh, convince him better."

Bobby stopped her abruptly, holding her in place with a rough hand. He looked her over carefully with a thorough eye. "Couldn't you have worn something more . . . enthusiastic, darlin'? I mean, if you want a man to have an unforgettable—"

"Not unforgettable that way, Bobby," she replied coldly. "I meant that he would really like going up. Maybe want to learn himself."

"Honey." Bobby smiled and put an arm around her shoulders. "You got a lot to learn about impressing a man. And not much time to learn it. I would've thought you'd know better by now."

"Never mind." She sighed, walking quickly across the level ground. "It'll work out. You'll see."

He looked skeptical. "I'll do what I can to help you, Ashley," he promised. "Not to make balloons anymore! That's awful."

"I know," she agreed with a small smile at his woeful expression.

"You could tuck that shirt in, Ashley," he suggested hopefully. "Show off . . . your beauty."

"Oh, Bobby!"

"Okay, okay. But I think I saw him admiring your . . . jeans yesterday."

"Bobby." She frowned murderously then glanced up at him. "You're crazy."

He laughed. "Nope. Just observant."

She laughed, too, as they approached the crew already getting the ropes ready and starting the cool air blowing into the balloon.

"Getting it ready for your inspection," Jeff Satterfield greeted her.

A few of the other men were people she recognized and she nodded to each of them. From the corner of her eye, she saw Trey reach their takeoff spot, standing off to the side, watching her.

"All right," she said to the crew, turning briefly to Bobby, her chief. "Let's go."

The balloon had puffed up from the big fan blowing into it, making a huge purple cave on the flat ground. Ashley walked into the envelope to inspect for tears or holes that might have been overlooked. It was a custom that had been continued since the beginning of ballooning. Her grandfather had taught her when she was just a child. She smiled when she remembered her grandfather telling her over and over that she had to trust her ground crew. His words rang true as she walked out of the envelope.

"Okay," she told them all. "Let's heat it up!"

The crew stood ready. Bobby nodded confidently to her. She didn't look at Trey but she could feel his eyes on her. She turned on the propane valve and lit the pilot light with her spark igniter then pulled on the blast valve. Bluish flames shot up from the burner through the balloon's gaping mouth. The temperature began to increase and the balloon struggled to rise from the ground. Bobby moved the fan out of the way and the rope handlers put extra tension on the lines to hold the balloon down.

Bobby and Jeff ran over to lean on the basket, calling to Trey to climb in. He scrambled over the edge and moved against the side across from where Ashley stood checking her pilot's gear.

Wrench, screwdriver, spare spark igniter. Bobby

handed her matches and a lighter just in case. A failed pilot light was a balloonist's worst enemy. She made sure the hundred-foot ground rope was coiled aboard, protective helmets dangling from the basket.

''Lucky quarter.'' Bobby flipped her a shiny silver coin. It was traditional for the phone call that might have to be made to the chase crew in case of emergency. ''Face the wind, darlin'.''

Trey watched the scene carefully. Especially Ashley. Between the rope and the instruments and straps, there wasn't much standing room. He moved a little, bumping his elbow on a helmet.

''Be careful not to touch the red strap,'' Ashley told him, not looking up. ''It spills hot air from the deflator port when we're ready to land.''

''Let's weigh off!'' Ashley called out. She timed a five-second burst from the blast valve.

Trey, waiting for the liftoff to leave his stomach on the ground, looked up and saw the sunshine filtering through the nylon balloon. It looked like a stained-glass window. He took a quick shot of the breathtaking sight. Max Spenser lifted his paper cup in salute.

Ashley looked at her watch, then used the blast valve once again and the roar echoed through the crowd. She held it open for about four seconds, then released it quickly. The silence was sudden after the noise of the flame. She glanced at Trey, finding his eyes resting on her then moving down slowly. Immediately, her gaze flew to Bobby's amused one.

"Have a good trip, honey," he yelled. "Watch your backside."

"What does that mean?" Trey wondered.

"Just, uh, balloon good luck," she answered with a shake of her head, watching Bobby laugh it off.

There was no sensation of movement but they were moving. When Trey looked, the people were moving away, waving to them and wishing them a good trip. He leaned over the basket slightly and the wicker creaked. He moved back. The balloon was drifting about twenty feet off the ground when a sudden shift of air currents sent it toward some trees.

"Ashley!" Trey caught her attention.

"Don't worry," she assured him. She put another blast of hot air into the envelope.

Nothing happened. The trees came closer.

"Ashley!"

"There's a ten- to fifteen-second time lag before the hot air gives us some lift," she told him calmly.

He eyed the trees warily. Slowly, the balloon began to rise, skimming the treetops. Trey was sure he could have reached down and picked a leaf.

"We'll go up to about five hundred feet," Ashley advised him, seeing his watchful gaze on the close ground below them. The balloon drifted with the breeze. Dogs barked up at them. People waved and took pictures.

"It's like we're not even moving," he said finally. "There's no breeze."

"Sometimes, you're just hanging up here. See the shadow?"

Trey looked down as some birds flew by just under the balloon. The sun cast their moving shadow on the green-and-orange clay ground below them. There was no blurring of the landscape. Just a steady motion. The balloon started drifting slowly downward, the landscape coming in closer as he snapped some pictures.

"Watch this," Ashley warned with a smile. She used a series of short bursts of heat to begin the climb up as they were nearing a red barn roof.

They drifted slowly skyward until Trey looked at the variometer and saw that they were rising at about two hundred feet per minute. There was only a mild elevator sensation on the bottom of his feet.

"We're leveling off at about fifteen hundred feet," she confirmed for him. She checked her fuel gauges and switched valves, changing to a full tank of fuel. "Wind's changed course." She nodded at the movement. "Maybe it'll blow us back to the airport."

"I'm sure your chase crew would like that." He smiled.

"It's great, isn't it?" she asked, not realizing how her blue eyes entreated him to find it so.

"Yeah." He didn't look away from her face, slightly pink from the sun, a few loose curls escaping from her ponytail. She could have been talking about drinking sewer water. He wouldn't have cared.

Ashley smiled a little wider. "I knew you'd like it." He was staring at her, she could feel it. "Is something wrong?'' she asked, a breathless catch in the back of her throat as she continued to feel his eyes on her.

"No." He shook his head slowly, then looked away to the horizon. "It's great. Really."

"You can see the chase crew down there." She pointed to the white RV pulling a purple-and-yellow trailer behind it. She glanced at her watch. "We'll land in about fifteen minutes."

"I would've never guessed it took so much," he told her. "I thought it was just up, up, and away. It's serious flying."

"The FAA is serious about it," she replied. "Every balloon has to pass inspection to be airworthy. That's one reason there's so few balloon makers left."

"And, of course, if you hadn't been set up to make the balloons, you couldn't make the nylon airbags," he continued.

"Exactly," she agreed. "That's how we made parachutes for the government before my grandfather died."

"Really?" He looked skyward into the purple nylon filled with air that suspended them in the bright blue sky. It looked unreal, as though it couldn't hold them up.

There was a sound like air sputtering, a noise that Ashley recognized at once. Nothing else sounded quite like it.

"Great," she whispered, and added a small prayer.

Chapter Eight

What is it?'' Trey wondered, seeing her go through her pocket, bringing out the spark igniter.

"The pilot's been blown out." She shrugged as though it were nothing. "Sometimes it happens." It was obvious after a few tries that the igniter wasn't going to light the gas pilot. "Hold this." She gave him the igniter and took out the failsafe matches and cigarette lighter.

Trey looked over the side of the basket. While there wasn't any feeling of losing altitude, the earth was definitely getting closer.

"Wind's changed again," Ashley observed calmly. She could tell that the balloon was going down. There would have to be an emergency landing. She tried to use the radio to call Bobby and let him know but there was only dead air. She would have to hope he noticed them drifting into the pretty valley below them.

"It won't light, will it?" Trey asked, looking back at her.

"No. Sometimes that happens," she answered truthfully. "There's nothing to panic about. We'll just go ahead and land. Bobby might have a little trouble placing us because this changes the flight plan but there's lots of houses down there. We'll be fine."

"Will we come down hard?" he questioned, wanting to know the worst.

"We shouldn't," she said honestly. "But you should face the direction we're landing and bend your knees to absorb the impact as we land."

"Okay," he acknowledged grimly.

"I'm afraid since we don't have a crew, you'll have to jump out when we reach the ground. I'll throw out the tow line and you'll have to make the balloon secure while I keep letting the air out."

He nodded. "Just let me know when."

"There's a clear spot there." Ashley pointed to a large field. It was open. There were no trees or power lines.

"No water," Trey added, concentrating on her words.

There were a few houses, and some outbuildings. Mostly it was tall green grass and golden flowers. The valley was sheltered between two small mountains topped with trees. A road ran straight through the middle and disappeared around the mountainside. From the balloon's height, a few thin clouds straggled above the treeline, but otherwise the sky was clear.

''With this wind,'' Ashley considered, ''we should come down just over there.''

''There's some trees within the rope's distance,'' Trey responded.

''I'm going to go ahead and send the rope over,'' she said, throwing the length over the edge of the basket. ''Get ready. We're coming up on landing.''

He nodded and when the basket touched the ground, he was out, over the lip and running with the rope toward the small copse of trees.

Ashley quickly deflated the envelope, the long ground rope catching the basket and balloon. The basket tilted, falling over as the weight from the nylon dragged it across the ground. But the fight was out of the balloon and it sank to the ground with a slight whistling sound. They made it down safely and the balloon was still intact. She looked around the fallen basket and saw Trey in much the same position that she was, sitting on the rocky ground, hands still clutching the rope. Her knees were a little shaky and she could feel the vibration in her hands.

''We made it,'' she said, hoping the experience hadn't soured the entire trip for him.

''What a ride!'' he yelled, falling back on the ground, letting go of the rope.

''Are you all right?'' she wondered, worried that he was hysterical.

He turned his head and looked at her. ''It was really

great! I didn't expect to like it. It's not something I ever wanted to do, you know? Sort of like closing your eyes and jumping off a cliff.''

Ashley laughed. ''I can't believe it! I thought you'd really want to close the balloon division down now.''

''Ashley,'' he said, getting to his feet, holding out his hand to her. ''I only said that to get you to take me up. Bannister *is* balloons!''

She stared at him. ''You were only kidding about the balloons not being profitable?''

''No, they aren't profitable. They could be more cost effective, but if the rest of the company is sound . . .''

''Why didn't you just tell me that you wanted to go up?''

''It wouldn't have been as fun as watching you trying to impress me,'' he remarked smugly.

''You are the most infuriating man!'' She would have picked up something and tossed it at him but her hands were too raw.

He saw the blisters on her palms and held his hands out. ''I suffered for it, too. Isn't there a first-aid kit?''

''In the gondola,'' she instructed. ''But we have to get the balloon picked up before it gets dark.''

''Let me get the first-aid kit and some gloves,'' he said, walking toward the basket. ''My hands aren't as bad as yours. Working with stone toughens you up.''

''Soft life,'' she chided, ''soft hands. I guess that's why you're so tough.''

He glanced back at her after righting the gondola.

"It would take more than tough hands to make you tough, Ashley."

She pushed her hair away from her face with the back of one of her injured hands. "You know, Rusty said pretty much the same thing to me. He thinks I'm not tough enough with you."

Trey scrounged through all the paraphernalia in the basket before finding the first-aid kit and two pairs of worn gloves. "Something about wolves in sheep's clothing?" he guessed, coming back to her.

"No, something like a lion and a lamb," she replied, starting to take the kit from him.

"Don't worry about it," he admonished, "and let the lion take care of it."

"I can do it," she began, but he was already taking out some gauze and some ointment.

He knelt in front of her on the coarse ground, looking into her face for a moment. "You're a difficult woman to help, Ashley Bannister. Put your hands out here, please."

She did as she was told, waiting quietly while he opened the ointment.

"I think this stuff might sting," he remarked casually, looking at the tube briefly before he smeared it on her open palms.

Ashley yelped and drew back her injured palms.

"I guess it does sting."

"You're all heart!" she told him, but after the first instant of pain, the numbing agent in the ointment kept her hands from hurting.

"I think we should put a bandage on each one or the gloves will make it worse again," he said, still gently swirling the ointment on her palms.

"All right," she agreed, feeling slightly uncomfortable in a way that had nothing to do with her rope burns. "Then I get to smear that stuff on *your* hands."

He cut a thin piece of gauze for each of her hands then wrapped it carefully around her palms.

"I'm not sure where we are." Ashley distracted herself from his touch by looking around them. Twilight was coming down rapidly, bringing shadows to the valley that hadn't been there even five minutes before.

"We must be on the map," he said logically. "There's a road."

"We can call from that house over there."

"There," he said, sitting back on his heels. "Feel better?"

"Much better. You would have been a good nurse. Now it's your turn."

He sat down and waited patiently while she cut two bandages and got out the tube of ointment. "My hands really aren't that bad," he said quietly.

She took one of his hands with both of hers and looked at it. "It looks as bad as mine. You'll need them to help with the balloon."

"Do your worst." He sighed as he felt her delicate touch on his hands.

Ashley stroked the cream on his palms, thinking about the beautiful things he'd created with those hands. His fingers were oval shaped, strong and sensitive. She trailed her touch down his hands and felt their power.

Trey wanted to touch her as she was touching him but didn't dare destroy the moment. It felt too good. He sat quiescently as she looked at his hands, wondering what she was thinking.

"You have beautiful hands," she said finally, then glanced up at him. "I mean, you do such beautiful things with your hands."

"Thanks on both counts," he answered softly. He pulled on a pair of the old gloves and flexed his fingers. "That feels better, Ashley. Thanks."

"I guess we better get started while we still have the light." She nodded, pulling her gaze away from his hands with an effort.

"Right." He walked purposefully towards the balloon, almost black in the near darkness.

It took only a few moments to fold up the balloon. There wasn't time to do the checks that usually went with getting the balloon ready to put away. They gathered the whole thing together then packed it carefully into the basket.

"I can call Bobby. He'll be waiting by the cell phone. We're probably just a few miles off course," she told him as they half carried, half dragged the basket with everything in it toward the farmhouse.

"No lights," Trey observed as they approached the house.

Ashley looked up. He was right. Not a light had

come on in the house although it was dark by the time they reached it.

"So, what now?" he asked, sitting on the stairs.

"We'll wait in the barn," she decided. "When we see a car come in the driveway, we can knock on the door and ask to use the phone."

"The barn?" he questioned, glancing at the large dark hulk.

"Unless you have a better idea?"

He shook his head. "The barn sounds fine to me."

"Okay." She picked up her side of the basket. "It shouldn't be too long."

Trey picked up his side. "Take your time, old son," he whispered privately to Bobby.

The barn was clean and sweet smelling with clover and hay. The stables were empty, although it was easy to see that they were normally in use. The water troughs were freshly filled and new feed had been put out.

A small, bare light bulb, half covered by a broken metal frame, provided all the light there was in the building. The rafters were high in the ceiling and covered by cobwebs, making heavy shadows along the barn floor.

"Just like home," Trey remarked, setting down his side of the basket.

"It's not so bad," she defended. "At least it's clean and dry."

It was like an omen. She had barely finished speaking when the light sound of rain started on the tin roof.

The wind picked up and a summer shower appeared to be settling in for the night.

"You must be psychic," he said, sitting down on a bale of hay near the door.

"We can leave the doors open. We'll see them when they come home and we'll just go up to the house," she detailed, sitting down on a bale close to him.

The rain became steady, heavy from time to time, but the barn was dry. Doves cooed in the rafters, fluttering their wings in the cool breeze.

Trey yawned and stretched, taking off his jacket. "Sorry. Rain always makes me tired."

"It's been a long day," she agreed stiffly. "If you'd like to go to sleep for a while, I could stand watch."

He looked at her skeptically. "I think I'm too hungry and thirsty to go to sleep."

Ashley went to the gondola. "There should be something in here that will help."

She pulled out the basket that had been packed for them. Inside was a small, white linen tablecloth, two crystal champagne glasses, and a bottle of champagne zipped into a cooler holder.

"You travel in style," Trey approved, moving closer to where she sat cross-legged on the barn floor.

"Always," she rejoined, spreading the cloth on a bale of hay and setting out the glasses.

There were a few chocolate mint cookies and a few cheese sticks. Ashley split the food while Trey opened the champagne. "Clever idea, packing a spread like this," he complimented.

The cork popped out and he poured the wine into the glasses. Ashley exchanged the food for her glass of champagne. "It's become part of the tradition," she explained. "When the first balloonists went up, they never knew where they would land. Sometimes the farmers and peasants thought they were devils when they came down. So to keep from being burned at the stake, they started taking a bottle of wine with them."

"Good idea," he considered thoughtfully. "Get the peasants drunk so they won't care if you're the devil."

"Exactly," she responded, taking a bite of her chocolate mint cookie. She felt a little awkward still wearing her gloves to protect her palms but they did keep them from hurting her. Ashley drank her champagne thirstily and Trey refilled her glass. They ate in silence for a few moments while the rain beat a steady tattoo on the roof.

She could feel his eyes on her and wondered what he saw when he looked at her.

With her hair scraped back from her face and not even a trace of lipstick, she guessed he was wondering what he was doing there with her.

She cleared her throat and started talking. The silence was getting the better of her. "There's a lot of tradition in ballooning," she told him, munching her cheese sticks, trying to ignore the lump in her throat. "It's more than just a sport or a hobby. It's like history being remembered every time a balloon goes up."

Trey poured himself another glass of champagne. "I was surprised how many balloons went up and how many people were there today."

"This is small!" she told him with unfeigned enthusiasm. "We went out west one summer—Phoenix, Arizona. The rally there was much bigger." She glanced across at him. "Some of our biggest balloon buyers are in California, you know. New Mexico—"

"I know," he nodded, carefully brushing crumbs from his hands. "I've read the sales reports." He didn't want to talk about sales reports or profit margins sitting there alone in the dark barn with her. The sweet smell of the rain reminded him of her perfume when he'd kissed her last night.

She smiled at him in the dim light, catching his eye. "You liked it, didn't you?"

"It was exciting," he admitted. "And impressive. It was like watching preparations being made for sending up the space shuttle!"

Ashley laughed. "You would've loved to watch my grandfather go up! It took him two hours to get the balloon ready. Everything had to be perfect."

"He must have been quite a character! Zeke and Bill and some of the others at the plant remember him so clearly. They seem to have skipped over your father," he remarked.

She twisted a loose strand of thread on the edge of the white tablecloth. "My father wasn't much of a balloon enthusiast. But he was a stickler for tradition."

"So," he surmised, "since the balloons were already in place, your grandfather continued to dictate the policy.''

''I've always thought my father was overshadowed by my grandfather. But he wasn't the kind of person who could strike out on his own. My grandfather was larger than life. He dwarfed everyone around him.''

''Everyone thinks you're like him, you know.'' He smiled, watching her animated face. ''A little young. A little wet behind the ears, to quote the notable stockholder Mrs. Jamison-Ross. Maybe in need of seasoning.''

''Seasoning?'' She shook her head, bemused. ''No matter what I do I'm always going to be little Miss Ashley.''

''That may be true,'' he agreed, moving slightly to ease down beside her against the hay bale. He split the last cookie with her and set his glass on the floor.

''All of my life I've tried to live up to everyone's expectations of me.'' She sighed. ''It's never enough.''

He leaned forward to look into her face. ''Ashley, you're smart. You run a multimillion-dollar company. Everyone who knows you thinks well of you. The only person it's not enough for is you.''

The rain was falling steadily, tapping lightly on the metal roof. The breeze that blew in from the open door brought in the sweet smell of summer rain, honeysuckle, and roses.

Ashley finished her cookie nervously, feeling the intensity of his appeal. In the dim light, his face was shadowed and his eyes dark. "What makes you say that?" she asked, her voice a trifle hoarse. She cleared her throat and faced him.

His hand encircled her wrist, taking the champagne glass from her unresisting fingers. "I know because you're me ten years ago. Always trying to live up to what other people think you should do. Never thinking about what makes you happy."

She shook her head. "I'm not like that," she argued, shivering as she felt his hand in her hair, freeing it from the confining hair clip. "I'm not afraid of being happy."

It was little more than a graceful gesture that brought his mouth to hers. His kiss barely grazed her, cool and sweet with the wine.

"I've just never been good at taking chances," she replied, the words coming out of her throat in a rush when he had moved his head.

There was a gleam in his eyes that was hypnotic and she felt as though she were drowning in it. He touched her cheek, gently stroked her hair from her face, and pulled her closer. "You haven't taken the right ones," he whispered against her throat. He kissed her gently, a finger lightly tracing her delicate ear.

Ashley felt as though she were drowning. His lips were as warm as the tender look in his eyes. The sensation surrounded her, threatening to engulf her completely. She panicked for an instant, tugging away.

It was the rain and the sound of the doves, the long

years when she thought she would never feel that way again, that were making her respond this way.

Yet even her feelings for Johnny hadn't been as strong. Nothing had ever felt so good, so right.

Trey took a deep breath, realizing suddenly where they were and what they were doing. He brought his spinning emotions—a part of himself that he thought had died ten years ago—under some slight control. "Sounds like a storm," he said in a voice he barely recognized as his own. He cleared his throat quickly.

"I guess it's good we found the barn anyway," she answered quietly, breathlessly. Her head rested against his chest.

Trey moved his hand down her back, wondering how he could think of letting her go. She smelled like summer sunshine.

A flash of near lightning made a blackened outline of the farmhouse against the night sky. A gust of wind blew in a cloud of rain, scattering hay and dust across the floor in circling devils.

Ashley sneezed and he offered a handkerchief.

"Are you all right?" he asked, when she had stopped sniffling.

"I'm fine." She smiled, embarrassed. "Probably just the dust."

"Ashley." He grinned, kissing her quickly. "I guess you were right. I am wicked. You made me this way."

"I didn't make you wicked, Trey," she reprimanded him. "You were already this way before I met you!"

"Then you make me abandoned. Crazy. Wild!" He stood up, taking her with him. A gentle hand slid down her neck, leaving her in no doubt that his need was as fierce as her own as he kissed her yet again.

She wrapped her arms around his neck and kissed his chin and the little scar near his mouth. "You are ruining my life," she told him, scrutinizing his laughing eyes, the tiny lines at the corners.

"And you are ruining my reputation," he retorted, swinging her around until she screamed for him to stop.

"What have I done?" she demanded breathlessly, blue eyes wide on his face.

"What have you done?" he repeated, his fingers sliding into her hair, his mouth coming down long and hard on hers until they were both trying to catch their breath. "You mean besides getting me to give up my normal life just to hang around you like some lovestruck puppy when I should be working?"

"I don't know what you mean," she answered, wondering if her lips could stop smiling.

"Since I saw you coming toward me in the diner, all I can think about is you. I've drawn your face a hundred times. I would've sewn the balloons myself just to be around you every day."

Ashley felt her eyes flutter closed as he leaned toward her, then felt cheated as his lips barely grazed hers.

"I didn't believe that I would ever feel this way again," she told him shyly. "Like the only reason to be with someone is because they make you feel alive."

Trey didn't smile. His eyes were fierce on her face. "As corny as that sounds, my life seemed fine until you weren't there for a few minutes. Then all I wanted to do was find you."

A loud clap of thunder shook the barn, the lightning hitting close by, zapping the power, leaving them in the blackness. The rain pounded down ruthlessly, pouring down the front of the barn like a river.

An unmistakable sound caught their attention.

"Do I know you?" the farmer asked from the other side of a long black shotgun.

Chapter Nine

It only took a few minutes to explain their problem to Emery Black and his wife, Harriet. They insisted on loading the balloon into their truck and taking them back up the mountain.

Trey and Ashley climbed into the backseat of the club cab behind the farmer and his wife and they set off for the airport. The roads leading away from the farm were muddy and dark. It took time to follow their treacherously narrow curves.

In the close darkness, Ashley felt Trey's warm hand slide across hers, entangling his fingers with hers. It was like a promise and she felt it deep inside her heart. At the end of the ride, there would be a complicated conversation. She wasn't sure yet what she would say to him. It seemed to have happened so quickly and yet it had been happening since they had first seen each other.

Did she love him? she wondered, looking out at the rain-swollen creeks they passed. She had only known him a short time. She had known Rusty all of her life.

It had been easy to be carried away with his kisses, with that feeling that she hadn't felt since she had first met Johnny. Being with Trey was an exciting roller-coaster ride. But when all was said and done, was it any more than that?

Trey hadn't mentioned love. That didn't surprise her. Ashley knew herself better. It wasn't that other men hadn't offered down through the years. While it was true that she felt something amazing for Trey, if it didn't include love, a relationship didn't interest her.

It was confusing, and in the darkness, with Trey sitting close beside her, it was difficult to think. One thing she was very clear on, as her conscience had continued to point out to her—she was not being fair to Rusty. She had practically told him that she would marry him. Her grandfather had always told her that honor was more important than success. If she was going to fall into Trey's arms every time they were alone, she would have to tell Rusty that she wouldn't marry him.

She didn't know if she was ready for that or even if she was capable of telling Rusty such a thing. He was more than just the man she was supposed to marry. He was a good friend. What would she say to him if he found out?

She was glad to see the lights of the rally through the mist that had risen with the rain. The downpour had actually stopped as they were coming up the mountain. There were still no stars visible in the night sky as they climbed out of the truck but the rally hadn't ended because of the weather. The fiddle player was still playing in the distance and the sound of singing was floating over the field.

"Stay and have something to eat," Ashley encouraged Harriet and Emery after thanking them for the ride.

"We'd like that," Harriet agreed, listening to the strains of the National Anthem.

"Looks like they're starting fireworks," Emery observed, getting out of the truck.

"What happened to you?" Bobby demanded fiercely. The rest of the team set about removing the balloon and gondola from the back of the truck. "Everything's soaking wet!"

"The pilot wouldn't relight," she answered, pushing a lock of hair from her eyes, wondering where she'd lost her hair clip. "We came down in a field."

"Heard that one!" Bobby laughed and slapped Trey on the back.

"Bobby! This is Harriet and Emery Black. Could you find them a couple of plates?" Ashley asked.

"Something sure does smell good," Emery admitted.

"I'm sure we can find something." Frances glanced

once at Ashley then walked away with the couple. "I'm Frances Anderson, Ashley's assistant."

"Do you know Genna Lambert?" Harriet asked her as they started toward the team RV. "You remind me so much of her."

"Lambert?" Frances mulled over the name. "We had a pastor at our church once named Lambert." Several aerial bombs exploded over their heads. The sound blocked out everything else. The red light from the sparkling umbrella cascaded down through the branches, quickly followed by a gold, then a green, shower of light.

"You did a mighty poor job packing that balloon," Bobby told her. "I think you must be out of practice, Ashley."

"You're probably right." she agreed, feeling awkward. Why hadn't Trey said anything? She wanted to look at him but wasn't sure what she would say to him.

"Remember how we were one short on the team?" Bobby continued, pulling on the bill of his baseball cap. "We're one short for the cleanup, too, young lady. You rode twice today with none of the dirty work."

"All right." She gave in, wishing he'd just go away. She felt like a twelve-year-old caught doing something she wasn't supposed to do. "Trey, I—"

"Ashley, I've got to talk with one or two people yet, then I'm heading back. I only brought one change of clothes.'' He smiled, the light from the rockets shimmering in the darkness of his hair.

Ashley was stung by his offhand words. She wished she could see his face.

''How was the ride, old son?'' Bobby wondered.

''Great.'' Trey shook his hand. ''It was like flying on a cloud.''

''That's the spirit.'' Bobby laughed. ''Ashley's a good pilot.''

''Count me in for next year's team.'' Trey shook the other man's hand. ''I've got experience now.''

Bobby turned back to Ashley as Trey started to walk away. ''The man loved it, honey!''

Ashley was tired and confused. ''I'm going to help them finish up.''

''Well, what about . . . ?'' Bobby let the question hang, with a slight head movement toward Trey's back.

''My feminine wiles?'' she scoffed. ''I'm better with machines.''

''Ashley,'' Bobby scolded as they walked arm in arm toward the balloon in the back of the truck. ''You just don't try hard enough. You're just not motivated.''

''I don't want to talk about it, Bobby,'' she retorted. ''I'm going to help pack this balloon, then I'm going home. You win that trophy tomorrow, okay?''

''Whatever you say, chief.'' He signaled her with a wry grin. ''I hope you got a place of honor for that trophy.''

It wasn't much of a job to lay the balloon out for the next morning's flight, especially with three other handlers. Bobby was nearly as demanding as her grandfather had been but they were still finished before the fireworks show was over. Ashley escaped the heavy traffic, leaving ahead of the crowd that waited until the last spark had died away. She refused to look back, ignoring the crowd and the lights.

Somewhere out there, Trey was wheeling and dealing. Harriet and Emery were eating and Frances was thinking of all the questions she was going to ask at the office Tuesday. Tired, wet and dirty, all Ashley wanted to do was get home. The long drive back seemed intolerable. She thought about spending the night at a hotel on the way back but decided against it. In the morning she was due at the plant to start working on the machines for Tagami. The drive wouldn't look any better in the gray morning light.

She turned on the radio and opened the car window, worried about staying awake. The rain had washed coolness into the heavily perfumed night air and the hum of the tires on the wet pavement was steady around her. She didn't want to think about what was happening between herself and Trey, concentrating on work instead, but that line of thought was full of pitfalls, too.

By inviting Trey in to help the company, she had opened the door to more than just possible financial success. He had Frances helping him to smuggle a new computer system into the plant. The stockholders loved him. David and Zeke thought he was the salt of the earth. When the time came, it wasn't going to be easy to simply tell him she didn't need him anymore. He was only slowly making himself indispensable.

She had to add herself to that list. It was good to have someone else think about the plant's finances. Just hearing herself think out loud was an invaluable tool. With Trey there, she felt she could concentrate more on the workings of the business and less on the profit margin. Of course, she didn't fool herself that he wouldn't get bored with the whole thing long before they were finished.

Despite her best intentions, she drifted back to the long moments in the barn. He made her laugh and feel good. What was she going to do?

She turned up the plaintive melody on the radio and sang along with it at the top of her lungs. The heavy traffic on the rainy highway whizzed by, the red taillights appearing to melt into the wet black pavement. The only thing she was certain of was something her father had taught her. You couldn't look the other way when it came to trouble. You had to face it—him— head on. She drove like a demon through the night.

The phone was ringing as she let herself into the dark, quiet house. She turned on a light as she closed the door and picked up the phone.

''I thought you'd be home.'' Rusty's voice took her by surprise.

After spending so much time on the way back thinking about Trey, she had expected him to be on the other end of the line. She wasn't disappointed, she told herself. Just surprised.

"Just walked in the door," she replied a little breathlessly, setting down her tote bag.

"I'm worried about you, Ashley. You seemed so preoccupied at the rally. I'm sorry I couldn't be there to drive you home."

"Thanks, Rusty." She shook her head. "I know you worry about me."

"But I won't so much after we're married," he told her confidently. "We've known each other for a long time, Ashley. I just want to take care of you."

"You know I don't want that," she answered quietly. "I've never been that kind of woman. You can't put me in your hip pocket, Rusty."

"I know that, honey. But we've always taken care of each other, haven't we?"

"Yes," she agreed in a whisper, his words evoking those early, almost forgotten years. She rubbed her eyes and wished she wouldn't have had to talk to him until she'd had a shower and eight hours sleep.

"I'll see you tomorrow, Ashley. We're going to be great together."

She looked at the ceiling, blinking back tears in her eyes. "I know, Rusty. Good night."

"Is there a problem, Ashley?" her mother asked from the staircase, startling her.

"No, Mother. I'm just tired. It's been a long day."

"That must have been quite a flight with Trey," she remarked, coming the rest of the way down the stairs, tying her peach-colored satin robe. ''When I left, you weren't back yet.''

''We lost the pilot light,'' Ashley replied in a dim monotone. ''I had to bring the balloon down and wait for a ride back.''

Margaret looked at her daughter carefully. ''You know, I believe I could do with a cup of hot cocoa. What about you?''

Ashley stared at her mother, a slow smile growing on her face. ''I don't think we've done that since I was sixteen.''

''I didn't think we would ever need to do it again,'' Margaret confessed with a sigh, continuing to walk toward the kitchen. ''But you always were a confused child.''

Ashley followed slowly, wondering what her mother had in mind. If she was going to lecture her, Ashley decided, she was going to bed.

''Sit down,'' Margaret instructed after she'd turned on the light.

Ashley sat at the wooden table with its neat floral centerpiece that her mother changed diligently with the seasons. There were so many things in the room that reminded her of her childhood. Doing her homework on the table while her mother made dinner, watching for her father to come up the walk from the garage.

''You're very attracted to Trey Harris, aren't you?''

''I find him attractive,'' she answered, skirting the real question. Had it been that long ago she'd sat at that table answering questions about her relationship with Johnny?

"And he finds you attractive," Margaret stated bluntly.

She emptied the packs of cocoa mix into two cups of water then put them in the microwave and closed the door. Ashley smiled when she thought about how much "cocoa times" had changed in the past twelve years.

"And what about Rusty?" her mother went on, getting out two saucers. The clock ticked and the timer chimed in the silence between them.

"I—I don't know, Mother."

"But you have led Rusty to believe that you're ready to marry him after all these years," Margaret observed, setting a cup, spoon and saucer before her on the table.

Ashley considered her words. "I've known Rusty all of my life. He's always been there for me."

"Sounds like an ideal husband." Margaret stirred her cocoa absently, her words hanging in the room.

"I know," Ashley agreed wearily. "And Trey couldn't be ideal, even if he wanted to."

"Does he?" Margaret asked bluntly. "Want to, I mean? Has he asked you to marry him?"

"No," she admitted honestly. "I don't expect him to ask me."

"What do you expect then?" her mother questioned patiently.

Ashley drank her cocoa and looked at her across the

table. ''I expect to save the company. Then I expect to retire gracefully to being a good wife and mother. I hope that will suit everyone?''

''If it suits you, Ashley.'' Her mother smiled, looking into her daughter's eyes, so like her own. ''I just don't want you to be hurt.''

''I know.'' Ashley got up and crossed around to the other side of the table to kiss her mother's perfumed cheek. ''I love you.''

''Good night, Ashley.'' Margaret cleared her throat. ''I love you, too.''

Halfway through the next morning, Ashley was sitting between two sewing machines, each nearly finished with the adaptations they needed to make Tagami's air bags. Her back hurt and she had grease all over her. She'd stuck her fingers twice with the fine needles as she inserted them into the machine head.

The plant was quiet around her as she continued to work, the occasional hum of a machine as she tested it breaking the total silence. David and Zeke had left for lunch with their families.

It was strange, she thought, looking up and around herself at the empty building. Everyone else looked at Bannister and saw the in and out of the money and they were right. But when she was alone in the building, she always heard the voices of the people who worked there. They were good people whose families depended on the paychecks they brought home every week. They came to the picnics and she cried at their weddings and funerals. They had cried at her father's funeral. She depended on their hard work as did the stockholders. Without them, there were no balloons, no reason to keep going.

Sitting on the cold cement floor, she thought about the times she remembered being there when her grandfather was alive. The company had meant everything to him. The business had passed down to her father because he was the only child but he never had the passion for it that his father had possessed. Ashley had grown up with the sounds of the machines and the smells of the grease. She'd taken naps on the huge piles of leftover nylon while balloons were being finished for races. It was so much a part of her, she didn't know if it was something she could give up to be anyone's wife.

What would she do? Marry Rusty and be a gracious hostess? Join the PTA and bake brownies? The business was important to her, the people and the balloons. Even the Tagami air bags and the yearly barbecues. Her grandfather had been part of the business and been a good father. The world wasn't what it was fifty years ago. Women did work, own business, and still managed to have families. How could she make Rusty understand what it meant to her?

"Ashley?"

She jumped, hitting her head on the side of the sewing machine.

"Sorry."

She groaned and rubbing her head then looked up into Trey's face. "What?"

"I called you from the doorway," he apologized. "I guess you didn't hear me."

"I guess not." She sighed, putting down the dirty rag she held and getting to her feet. She looked at him again, a little annoyed to be standing there in a greasy pair of shorts and a T-shirt two sizes too big. "What are you doing here?" she asked, surveying his well-pressed dark slacks and carefully buttoned pale green shirt with a critical eye.

"I just got back from sweet-talking the last of the stockholders. I think we're okay for a while. At least, everyone seems willing to give us a chance."

"Give *you* a chance, you mean," she muttered, pulling up a chair to the sewing machine she'd just finished repairing.

"They wouldn't have bought it without you being there as well," he countered.

"Thanks." She ran a piece of nylon through the machine. The silky white material slipped through, stitches neatly in a row. Ashley stood and arched her back with a groan.

"I think I can help that," he volunteered. Long, deft fingers massaged her spine.

"That's wonderful," she murmured, closing her eyes.

"You have to thank my brother-in-law, the chiropractor. My sister married him for these skills."

"Do you only have one sister?" she wondered.

"I had a brother but he died when I was six," he told her quietly. His words echoed strangely in the silence of the brightly lit plant. "He was hit by a car on the way to the park."

"I'm sorry. I know your sister must be glad you came back."

"We're pretty close," he agreed. "I just became an uncle last year."

She smiled and shook her head. "I would never have guessed you were a family man."

"There's a lot you don't know about me, Ashley. Despite Frances's snooping," he told her, his eyes lingering on her lips. "You managed to run away pretty quickly last night."

"We both had things to do," she retorted as quickly.

"I think we should talk, Ashley." There was no mistaking the set of his mouth or the intent in his eyes.

"I don't know what there is to say," she replied carefully, moving away from him.

"I can think of a few things," he explained, catching her off guard as he moved his arm around her waist. He kissed her slowly.

She stood in the circle of his arm and felt all the opposition leave her body. He was close enough to lean against and she did, shamelessly, wrapping her own arms around his neck. "I'm full of grease," she protested halfheartedly, barely moving back an inch from his mouth. It was a little late but she suddenly remembered all her good intentions from the previous night.

"I'm wearing washable clothes," he replied, kissing her again.

"I thought you said we should talk," she said, trying to catch her breath. The whirlwind he created in her was painful in its intensity.

Trey laughed, a deep rumbling she heard in his chest. His hands moved surely up and down her spine, bringing her closer to him. "You know, every ridge in your back has a specific function," he began in a voice that made her tingle. "When you touch here"—he proceeded to show her—"it relaxes your neck and shoulders."

Ashley already felt like limp nylon. She closed her eyes and enjoyed the massage.

"Here"—he massaged a spot in her lower back—"reduces stress and improves circulation to your legs and hips."

Ashley made a faint protest that he silenced with his mouth on hers. A faint sound brought Ashley back to her senses. What was she doing? "Trey," she whispered, her voice catching on his name.

"Hmm?"

"Trey," she managed a little louder. "We . . . this . . . can't go on."

"What do you mean?" he asked softly, pulling back his head to look at her. Her hair was a mess and there didn't appear to be a place on her without grease but she made his blood pressure soar.

"I mean that I'm going to marry Rusty," she told him a little more strongly though she hated to have him move his arms from around her. "Maybe not right now but someday."

He searched her face. "I thought we agreed yesterday that we have something special between us."

Ashley squirmed and he let her go. She picked up a wrench that she'd left on the floor and put it back into the tool box. "I've known Rusty all my life. He was there when I graduated from high school and there when Johnny dumped me. He's always been there for me. I owe him something more than this."

"Then tell him." Trey shrugged. "Tell him he's been a good friend but that you love me."

Ashley turned around and looked at him in disbelief. "I can't do that."

His warm eyes had begun to take on a decided chill. "Why?"

"Because I haven't known you long enough to know if I love you," she replied in good sense. "I find you attractive."

"Ashley." He held up one hand. "How long has it been since you broke up with Johnny?

She shrugged. "Ten years, but I—"

"How many men have there been in your life?"

She colored slightly. "Well, none, really, but I—"

"You've never felt about Rusty the way you feel about me. I've seen you with him. I've seen you kiss him. What we feel isn't something that comes along every day. I know. I've tried to find it."

"Trey." She stopped him as he would have taken her in his arms again. "This isn't right. I can't throw everything away for something that may only be a short fling."

He let his hands drop from her arms and stepped back from her. "Maybe I'm wrong. I thought there was more to this than that. A short fling, huh?" His eyes swept over her with devastating intensity.

"I told you," she reiterated. "I'm not good at taking risks. I've always been better at the straight-and-narrow course. I'm sorry."

"So am I." He turned and started to walk away from her and she felt something sink in the pit of her stomach.

Suddenly he turned back and brought her up hard against him. Their faces were close enough that she could see the glittering depth of his eyes. "Tell me that you don't love me, Ashley Bannister! In your own words. Take your time. Tell me that you don't want me to hold you, that you don't know the minute I walk into a room. Can you do that?"

She stared into his eyes, saw the fierce need in him that she felt within herself and opened her mouth to speak but no words formed on her lips.

"That's what I thought." He let her go. "Go look at yourself in the mirror, Ashley. Kiss Rusty. It's a long life. Think about it."

Chapter Ten

Ashley watched him walk out of the plant, closing the door quietly behind him. The sunlight danced across him for an instant as he stood in the doorway, then he was gone.

She put her hand to her mouth. Her heart was pounding. It was frightening what the man did to her. Even after he'd left her, she could still feel his touch. She was a sane, sensible person. Or at least, she had always thought so. She didn't love him, couldn't love him. Yet something was dying inside of her.

Had he said that he loved her? Her mind searched back through his words. He'd said that they had something special. Was that love? Or was it his bright eyes and his easy laugh? Was it his clever words? Or his way of making her feel as though she was more than just "little Miss Ashley." Was there something about the way he walked or the way he held his head or the sinewy strength of his hands?

Was that love? The only love she could honestly recall having was Johnny. He was everything to her. She would have given up anything to be with him. She would have done almost anything he had asked of her. Yet in the end, he'd left her.

Maybe she had never really loved Johnny. Maybe that was infatuation and it had quickly died for him. What she felt for Trey was too confusing, coming at a time when her life was already confused and uncertain. How could she really know what she felt for him? But if she did love Trey, could she let him go because it seemed to be the right thing to do? As her mother was fond of reminding her, she wasn't getting any younger. Could she afford to let a chance for happiness pass her?

She picked up a wrench and put it back down. Her hand was shaking. Nothing was right. It didn't take much soul searching to admit that she had never loved Rusty. She had made that clear to him. He'd told her that it didn't matter. They liked each other well enough and they had roots. She had agreed, telling herself that what she'd felt when she was eighteen would never come again. She could marry Rusty. They could have a family. Her life could be good.

Yet Trey had kissed her and made her laugh and dared her to deny the fire between them. Maybe there was something to be said for taking chances. Could she hurt Rusty that way? How could she tell him? How could she not?

She didn't have long to consider it. Only a few minutes later, Rusty knocked on the window and waved to her. She put down the pressure foot she'd just taken off the machine and watched him as he came into the plant.

"Hi, honey. Ready?" he wondered, his smile steady and strong on his face.

She found herself looking at him as though she'd never seen him before, searching his strong profile for . . . something. What? she questioned. Rusty was himself. He had always been the same. He didn't understand sarcasm, liked bluegrass music, and ate the same breakfast every morning. His ties didn't match his shirts.

There was no one else to see. Plainly, if she were looking for Trey, she would not find him in Rusty.

"I thought we'd go to the drive-in down at the corner. I'm sure you'd rather not change until you're finished." He glanced down at his own checkered green shorts and faded blue shirt then up at her grease-stained clothes.

Ashley smiled at him and pushed the disturbing thoughts from her mind. "Thanks. I'll just be a minute."

"So, how are things going?" he asked, sounding interested.

"Pretty well," she answered, surprised that he

asked since she knew his opinion of her working on the machines.

"Great!" He grinned, following her into the office. "That's really great."

While she washed in the small bathroom, Rusty told her about the progress they were making in the Turner estate. "Lucky thing for us that it was a long weekend," he mused. "What a mess."

"Is all that legal, Rusty?" she wondered seriously.

"Of course," he retorted strongly. "We wouldn't be involved otherwise. We're a reputable firm."

They had lunch. Rusty dominated the conversation, telling her about his morning between bites of onion ring. When he'd finished his lunch, he turned to her. "How would you feel about a late summer wedding, honey?"

Ashley put aside her half-eaten sandwich. What she had eaten felt like a rock in the pit of her stomach. "I need more time, Rusty. The plant—"

"You're giving up the plant. Don't forget that. I know you want it to be doing as well as possible so you can get a good price for it."

"I don't think I can do that, Rusty," she managed to tell him calmly. "It's my grandfather's blood, I guess. You're going to have to love me as a working wife."

He gripped the steering wheel hard. "I saw you, Ashley. With him."

She looked out the window. "I'm sorry, Rusty."

"Do you love him, Ashley?"

"I think I do." She sighed. "It wasn't something that I expected."

"Does he love you? Or is this another relationship like the one you had with Johnny?"

"I don't know," she answered truthfully. "He hasn't told me that he loves me."

"We've known each other for so long," he protested. "We could have been so good together."

Ashley smiled and touched his hand. "I think we should both be looking for more than that, Rusty. Just because we're comfortable with each other, doesn't mean we love each other."

"I love you," he answered fiercely.

"I love you, too," she agreed. "But I think it must not be enough or we would have done something about it years ago."

"Maybe you're right," he half agreed. He looked at her. "But sometimes, it's better to be comfortable than brokenhearted."

Ashley smiled and wiped a tear from the corner of her eye. "I don't deserve you."

"That's true." He laughed, hugging her to him. "Has he asked you to marry him?"

"No," she told him shakily. "There hasn't been anything like that between us."

"Well, if he doesn't come up to snuff, I'll sit on him for you."

"Thanks, Rusty." She sniffled and wiped at her eyes. "Will you be okay?"

"In a way," he admitted, "it's a relief. Kissing you

is a lot like kissing my sister, Ashley. I thought there was something wrong with me.''

They laughed together and held each other. ''My mother is going to be so disappointed,'' Ashley told him.

''Mine, too,'' he told her. ''Better them than us, though, huh?''

Ashley went through the motions of doing her job when Rusty took her back to the plant but her mind and her hands refused to work together. David and Zeke came back from lunch but didn't act as though they noticed any difference in her. It made her want to laugh out loud and cry at the same time. She had cut her ties with the past without knowing if there was a future for her with Trey. It was fair. Rusty deserved to find someone who could really love him. She deserved the same.

She went home the same way. Not really thinking yet thinking about everything that had happened to her. It was as though she had rounded a bend in the road and she couldn't go back again. But how did she go forward?

She lay in the darkness that night, trying to sleep. She was exhausted but filled with too much nervous emotion to close her eyes. Her life of the past ten years rolled out before her like a movie played on her ceiling. She had thought at one time, when Johnny had left her, that it was going to be the end of her life. She had sobbed herself to sleep many nights after he was gone, a pillow over her head so that no one could hear her crying.

This time it was much worse. There were no tears to bring her solace and no huge gaping wound that she felt sure would tear her apart. Just a feeling of loss. A quiet haunting agony too deep for tears. And a feeling that, once more, she had been wrong. Maybe she had been born to be alone, she reflected in that darkness. Johnny had been gone for ten years and she had managed to live alone.

Trey isn't gone yet, a tiny voice nagged at her. *There is still time.*

Fear and pride silenced that small voice. If it hurt that much to lose him and they hadn't had a relationship, what would it be like to have lived with him? Perhaps to have had his children?

Trey was right. She was a coward. She admitted it. She was afraid to think what would happen if it didn't work out. What if she wanted more from Trey than he could give her? She was afraid she might never find her way out of that darkness.

She fell asleep as the sky was tinged with pink and the birds had started to call for the sun. It was sometime later, after a dozen phone calls from the office, that Margaret knocked on the door. Not hearing anything from within, she entered her room.

She couldn't recall the last time she'd seen her daughter asleep. Usually she was up hours before Margaret herself. Following her grandfather, talking business with her father, running the plant. Mother and daughter seemed destined to go their separate ways. In sleep, her usually animated face composed, Margaret saw the features of that little girl that she never really understood but tried her best to love.

She wasn't the prissy little girl her mother had wanted, all lace and pretty little dresses. But she was a wonderful person, loyal and brave. Margaret admired her daughter more than she was able to tell Ashley. She would have killed anyone who tried to hurt her or stand in her way.

''Ashley,'' she called, hating to give up that minute in her shaded bedroom.

Ashley rolled over and mumbled something unintelligible.

''Ashley,'' her mother called again, this time touching her placid face.

In the instant between sleeping and waking, Ashley remembered another time when she'd been sick and her mother's cool, smooth hand had touched her fevered cheek. She opened her eyes and saw her mother's anxious face, her makeup perfect as always. Had she ever seen her when it wasn't?

''What time is it?'' she questioned quickly.

''About nine-thirty,'' Margaret told her with a small smile. ''Everyone in the free world is looking for you. Bad night?''

''You could say that,'' she replied, starting to get up. Her head felt like it was stuffed with cotton and for all of her late night reveries, she still didn't know what to do.

"Sorry." Her mother arched a perfectly shaped brow. "Have a little something to eat before you go. Maybe some juice."

"I don't think I could eat anything," Ashley muttered, dragging her tired body to the bathroom.

"How bad could it be?" her mother asked, sitting on the bed, waiting. "What's happened anyway?"

Ashley couldn't face her mother with it, so she told her everything from the bathroom as she washed her face and brushed her teeth. "I know you're disappointed," she finished before she walked out of the bathroom. "But I believe it's for the best."

"Ashley, I think you love Trey. And I think he obviously cares for you."

Ashley walked out of the bathroom and stared down at her mother. "What are you saying? I thought you wanted me to marry Rusty. Do you think I should have a relationship with Trey?"

"Just a relationship?" Her mother was aghast. "No, indeed. I'm saying that you should marry the man. If he has anything else in mind, you need to set him straight."

"I'm not sure what he has in mind," Ashley whispered. "And I'm afraid of making a mistake again."

Margaret took her daughter in her arms and looked into her tired face. "Maybe you don't know him very well. But you love him, don't you?"

Ashley nodded, not trusting herself to speak.

"Then you go after him and you take your chances, Ashley. I wasn't sure about marrying your father either. He and I were very different but we loved each other for thirty-two years. Don't let that mistake you made with Johnny ruin the rest of your life.''

''Thanks, Mom,'' Ashley cried, leaning against her fragile mother.

''Take care of that face. Have some coffee. Everyone else will wait.'' Margaret counseled.

It was the housekeeper's day off, so when the doorbell rang, Margaret knocked on the bathroom door and told Ashley she would wait for her downstairs.

Ashley showered and dressed, using makeup with a more lavish hand than usual. She decided against pulling her hair back from her face, instead choosing to leave it loose and curling slightly at her shoulders.

It was about time to visit the hairdresser. She made a mental note. She didn't like her hair to get too long. It tended to curl and required too much attention. She checked her pale blue suit and white silk blouse again, slipping her feet into matching blue flats. She clipped expensive gold earrings on her ears. They had been a gift from her grandfather when she had turned fourteen. Maybe they would give her some courage.

She looked at herself in the mirror, seeing the worried frown between her eyes, the tense line of her mouth. She was worried and tense, she told herself crankily. What had she expected?

Going carefully down the long stairway, she wondered who had been at the door. Her mother had disappeared and the house was quiet. If she was lucky, she would be able to slip out before her mother tried to make her eat breakfast.

"Ashley," Margaret called out from the library just as her daughter's hand was on the door knob.

"I'm late, Mother," Ashley told her, not looking back.

"I know, dear, but there's something you should see."

Ashley turned around slowly, not sure she could handle anything else. Her heart beat fast. Had Rusty changed his mind and decided to try and change hers as well?

She walked into the library warily but it was empty except for her mother.

"Look at this," Margaret invited, lovingly touching a sculpture that was barely unwrapped from a packing crate.

"Where did this come from?" Ashley asked, holding her breath as she looked at the beautiful work.

"A delivery driver just left it," her mother explained.

Ashley studied the sculpture, feeling as though she were looking in the mirror.

"He captured that look in your face," her mother mused. "Your father used to call it your dreaming look."

Ashley looked at the signature at the base, not surprised at the artist's name. She marveled at the curve of the cheek and the hope she saw in her double's eyes. Was that really what Trey saw when he looked at her?

"I don't think you have to wonder what that man feels for you, Ashley." Her mother sighed, beginning to dream about a house full of grandchildren. "I thought his other work was good, but this—this is exquisite."

The tears that she had promised herself she wouldn't cry were sliding down her face. Trey had managed to put his feeling for her into the clay he'd molded to resemble her. She understood that he was trying to show her what he saw when he looked at her, when he kissed her.

"He's made me look . . . beautiful." She touched the statue, feeling a sudden sense of well-being. Her world had tilted but he had righted it. She had no choice. She had to believe in him.

"I have to go." She hugged her mother and ran for the door.

"Be careful, Ashley!" Her mother called out behind her.

Ashley drove to Trey's farm with her foot down hard on the gas pedal. If there had been any police out on the roads she flew down that hot summer morning, they would have surely pulled her over and ticketed her. She didn't care. Heart racing, afraid that there wouldn't be another chance, she kept her eyes on the road and her destination in her heart.

A distant tongue of lightning caught her attention as if forked to the ground. The hot weather had brought a storm but it was nothing like what raged inside of her. The heavy humidity had turned to a strong downpour before she left Martinsville. Steam rolled up from the streets as thunder rolled across the countryside. People, caught unaware, scurried for shelter from the wind and rain.

It was a long drive out to his house. It was hard for her to tell where the rain began on her windshield and where her tears ended. She thought over every word, every nuance, that had passed between them. She had thought her heart was dead but it bloomed within her. Sometimes, you had to walk too close to the edge to see the truth.

Ashley parked on the side of the road. She wasn't sure if she could find the words. She could still walk back down and he would never know. She walked up, drenched by the time she reached his front door. The house was silent and empty. The dogs didn't bark.

She asked herself, repeatedly, what she was going to say to him. *"Kiss Rusty,"* he'd said, *"then take a look in the mirror."* She didn't have to look in the mirror, though. He'd sent the truth to her, lovingly created in her own eyes.

She wasn't sure how long she stood out there in the rain, looking at the house, wondering what he would think if he knew that she was outside.

Lightning flashed around her and the sky turned an ominous black. She looked up at the sky then at the dragon on the chain. If she were hit by lightning, he would never know, she reasoned at last, urging herself to move. He would think that she had abandoned him. Like Johnny had abandoned her. Where had he found the courage to send her that statue after she had rejected him? How had he managed to fight his way free of the fear?

"Trey?" she yelled, knocking on the front door. She heard the dogs barking somewhere outside the house but couldn't see them. There was no answer. She walked around to the back of the house and caught sight of his white stucco studio near the barn.

Rain played with a skillfully created dolphin who jumped in a pool in the center of the neatly trimmed yard. The rain brought the scent of roses and herbs growing around her. In the nooks and crannies of the white gravel path were tiny creatures, some recognizable, others purely imagination.

Ashley skirted the edge of the water and pushed her rain soaked hair out of her face, trying to build up the courage to open the door to the studio. *He'll probably think I'm crazy,* she guessed. Maybe she was, just a little. She had barely slept, hadn't eaten since the day before and her heart was pounding like it would burst from her chest. Her hair was dripping down in her eyes and she shivered in her ruined blue suit. Her shoes were covered with wet sand.

Trying not to think about what she would look like to him, she pushed open the door to the studio and stood, dripping rain, on the black tile floor.

He didn't look up, though the dogs ran to greet her. He was drawing something on a large pad of paper, flipping over pages quickly as his hand flew across the bare sheets. He was wearing heavy, dark-rimmed glasses. His hair was loose on his shoulders and looked as though he'd been running his hands through it. His face was dark with a new growth of beard. It reminded her of the day he'd come to her office to tell her that he would help her save the plant.

He glanced up, surprised to see her. "Ashley?"

"Hi," she returned weakly.

He stared at her for a long moment. It hardly made sense that she would be standing there, soaked to the skin, staring back at him. "What are you doing here?" he asked, wondering what had happened to her.

"I, uh, just came by to, um, tell you that your stocks will be transferred tomorrow."

Those dramatic, light eyes, that had embraced her with their warmth, held shades and shadows of pain and, she hoped, love. *Please let him love me, just a little*.

"Thanks," he replied. "But you didn't have to walk up here in the rain. A phone call would have done just as well."

"I know," she answered. "I just, well—"

"Would you like some coffee . . . and a towel?" He tried to push his way past the surprise at seeing her there. He had imagined it so many times that it didn't seem real.

"Thanks." She peeled off her suit jacket, shivering. "I'm sorry about the water."

"Don't worry about it," he remarked. "Maybe I

should make that a blanket. Or better yet, my sister is always forgetting some of her clothes here.''

''No, that's all right. I'm not staying. I only came out to tell you about the stocks.''

''Why are you here, Ashley?'' he asked, handing her a green towel from a cupboard behind him. ''And don't tell me you ruined your clothes to tell me about stocks.''

She took the towel and wrapped it around her shoulders, glancing around the room that was so like him. Organized. Not a sign of clutter. Drawings and sculptures everywhere. Thunder boomed like a death knell and she shuddered. It was the moment of truth.

''I got the sculpture,'' she blurted out.

He nodded and looked away from her rain-washed face. ''I'm glad.''

''When did you have time? I mean, I didn't even sit for it.''

''You didn't need to,'' he replied softly. ''I've spent a lot of time looking at your face, Ashley.'' He didn't look at her.

''Trey, I know I was wrong. I know that I should have trusted you. I'm sorry.'' The words gushed out of her all at one time as she stood looking at him over the books and papers that were stacked on his desk.

He folded his arms across his chest. His black T-shirt and jeans had seen better days. They were threadbare and fit him like a second skin. He had a smudge on his chin and a pencil tucked behind his ear.

''Ashley—''

"I learned something when I looked at the sculpture," she told him, bravely deciding to go for broke.

He glanced at her, hardly daring to breathe. Calmly, he took off his glasses and laid them down on the table. His hands were shaking when he looked up at her. "What did you learn, Ashley?"

"I know that you love me," she whispered. "I saw it in the sculpture. When you touched that clay, you were pretending that you were touching me."

He crossed the small space between them and stared down into her face to see the truth for himself in her expressive eyes. Then he wrapped his arms around her, absorbing the chill of her body with his warmth.

"I love you. I don't want to lose you." she continued, holding tightly to him.

"Not in this lifetime, Ashley." He kissed her, his mouth warm and safe on her own cold lips. His touch caught fire and changed, making her warm despite her wet clothes.

"I love you, Ashley," he murmured, kissing her ear.

"Trey," she muttered darkly, "you were right. I was a coward."

"A beautiful coward," he replied, kissing her wet face. "With the bluest eyes in the world. That was the one thing that bothered me. The sculpture couldn't reflect your eyes."

"It was wonderful," she complimented. "You're wonderful."

He kissed her. "What about Rusty?"

"I talked to him," she told him.

"What did he say?" he asked politely.

"He said that kissing me was like kissing his sister." She laughed. "I think he might be happier with someone else."

Trey framed her face in his hands, stroking her smooth skin with his fingers. "I think you might be happier with someone else, too, Ashley."

"Someone like you?" she murmured.

"Someone just like me," he answered, kissing her lovingly. "But I am a risk. Can you trust me? Will you marry me?"

"I have to." She smiled and sniffed. "I don't know how to live without you anymore."

"Then it will be an adventure the likes of which no balloon ride has ever been," he promised dramatically. "Because I never want to live without you again, either."

"I love you," she repeated, beginning to feel much warmer.

"Take a chance then, Ashley," he urged in a husky voice. "Kiss me."

"Anytime." She folded her arms around his neck. "Anywhere."